JAKE MADDOX
GRAPHIC NOVELS

DAYDREAM RECEIVER

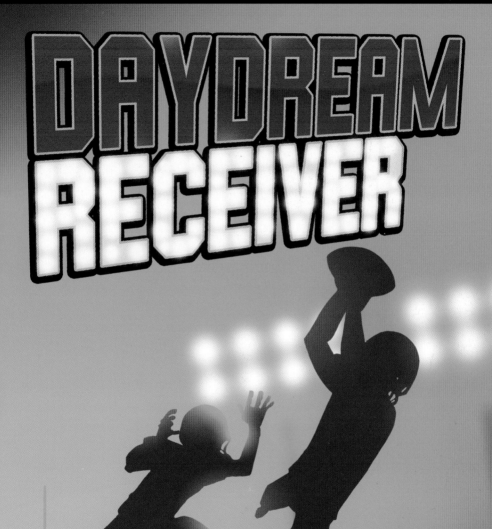

STONE ARCH BOOKS
a capstone imprint

JAKE MADDOX
GRAPHIC NOVELS

Jake Maddox Graphic Novels are published by
Stone Arch Books, a Capstone imprint
1710 Roe Crest Drive
North Mankato, Minnesota 56003

www.mycapstone.com

Library of Congress Cataloging-in-Publication Data is available on the Library of Congress website.

ISBN: 978-1-4965-3702-7 (library binding)
ISBN: 978-1-4965-3706-5 (paperback)
ISBN: 978-1-4965-3722-5 (ebook PDF)

Summary: Gus Blackburn is a dreamer. He dreams of catching the winning touchdown in the big game. He dreams of being as popular as the team quarterback, and of smooth talking with the girls in his school. But in reality Gus is an oversized, third-string receiver who rides the pine more than running routes on the field. However, with the homecoming game fast approaching, Gus is determined to show his teammates that his size won't keep him from living out his dreams.

Editor: Aaron Sautter
Designer: Brann Garvey
Production: Gene Bentdahl

Printed in the United States of America.
010044S17

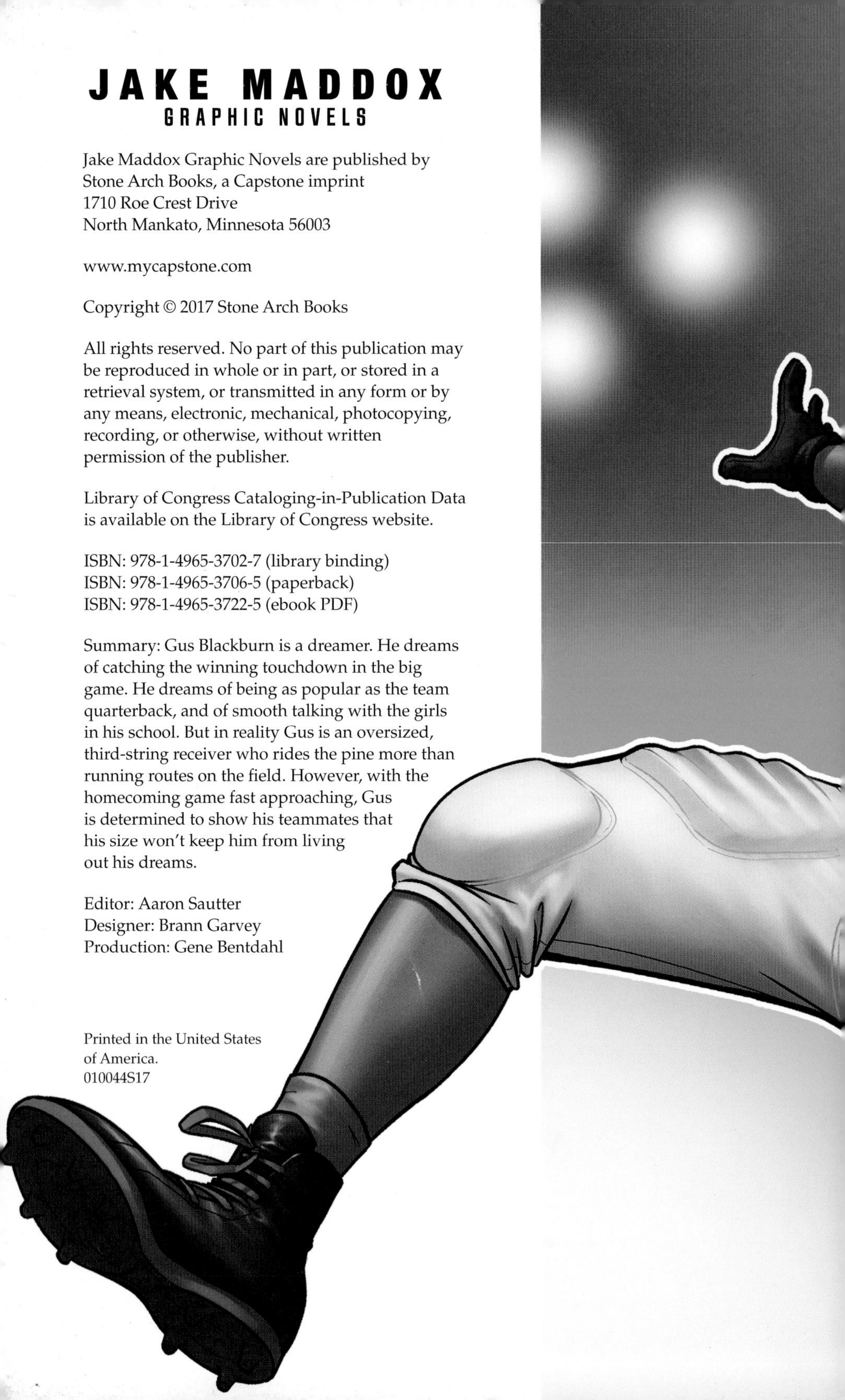

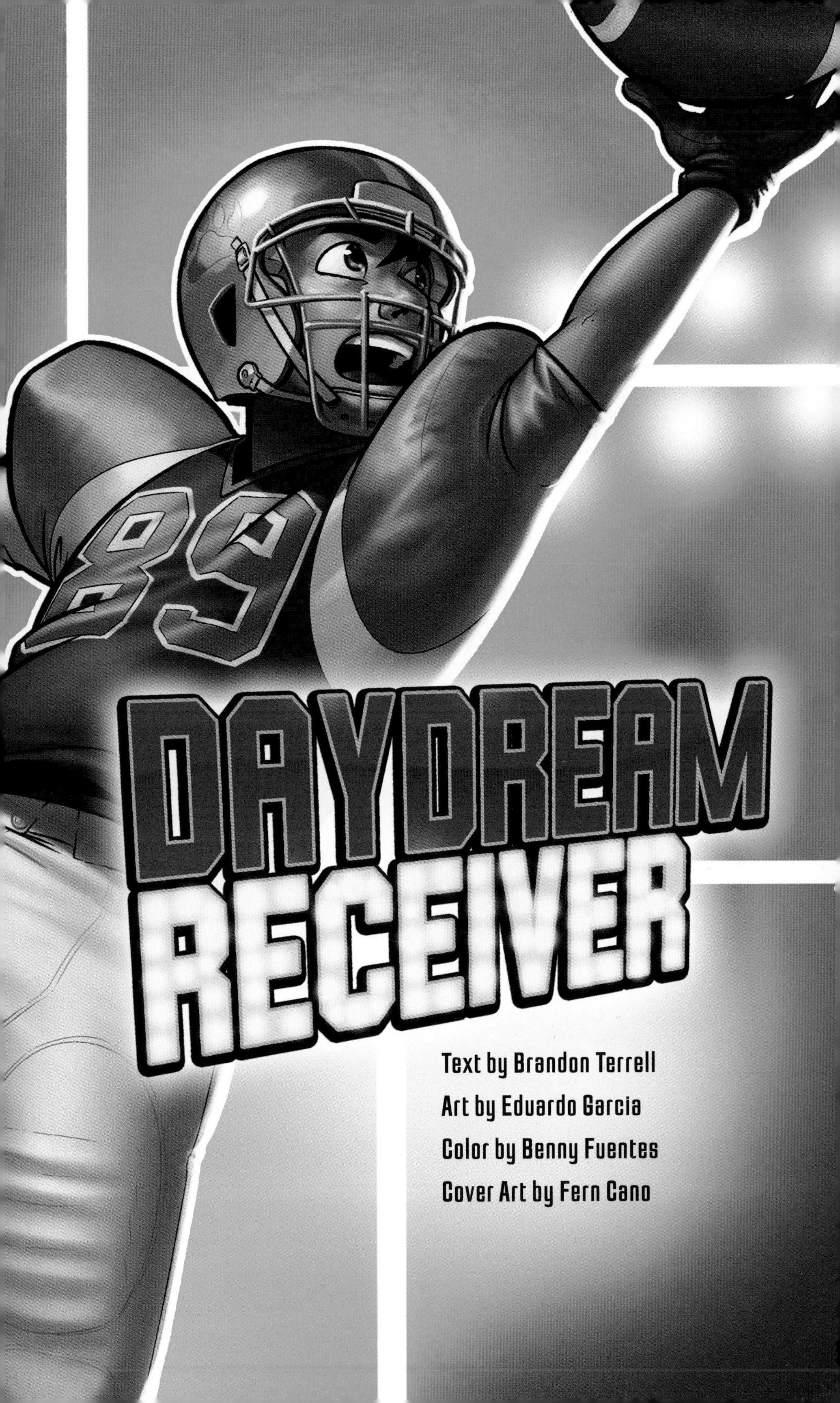

DAYDREAM RECEIVER

Text by Brandon Terrell

Art by Eduardo Garcia

Color by Benny Fuentes

Cover Art by Fern Cano

THE STARTING LINEUP

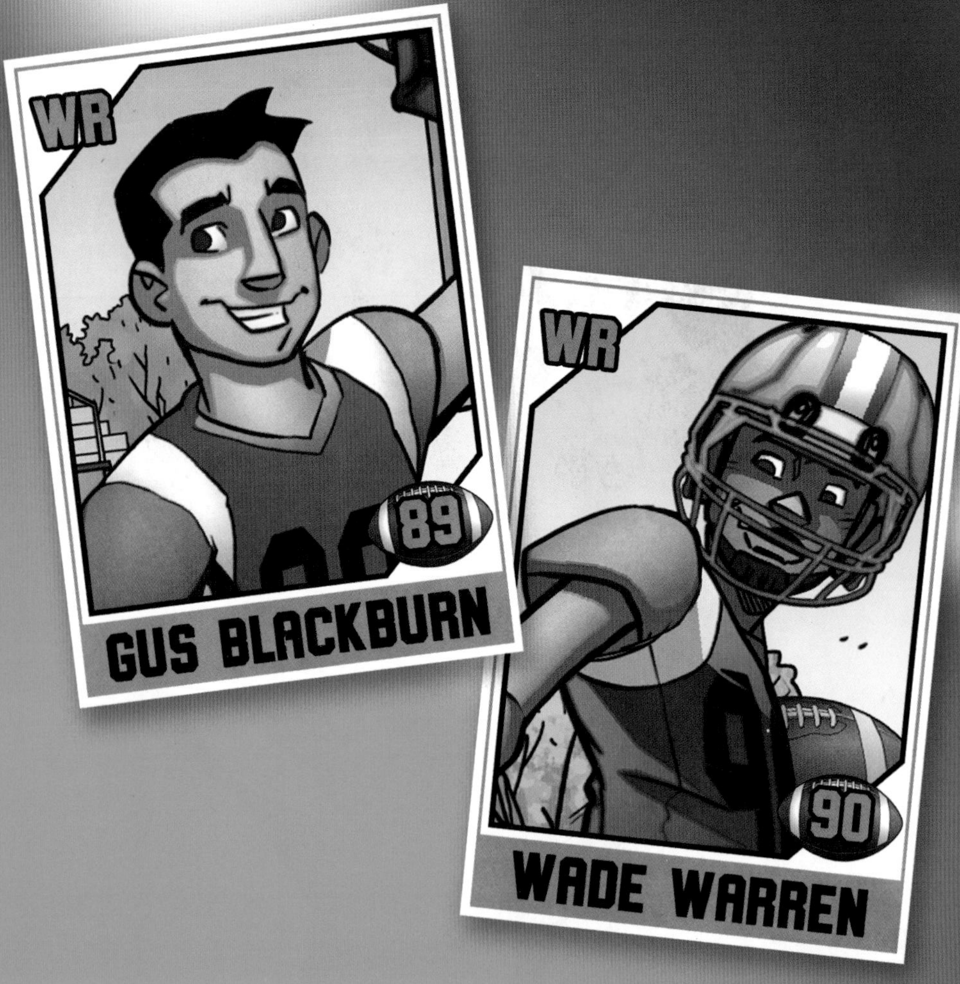

WR
89
GUS BLACKBURN
WR
90
WADE WARREN

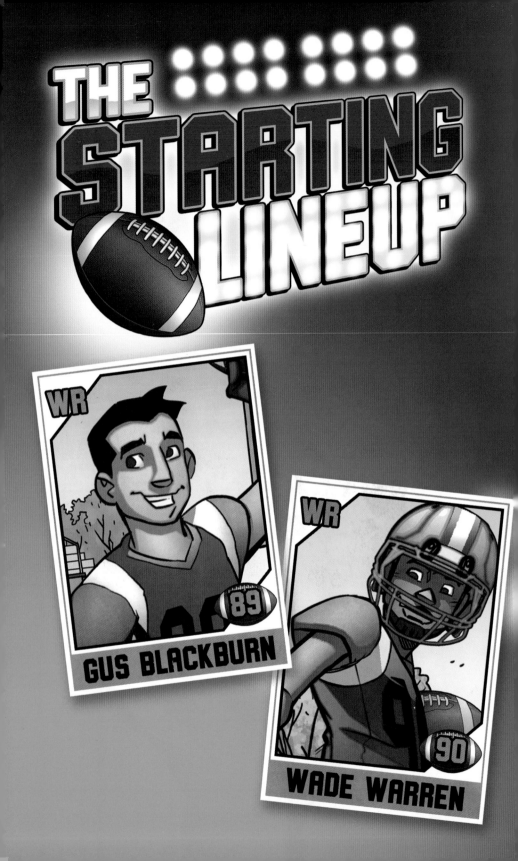

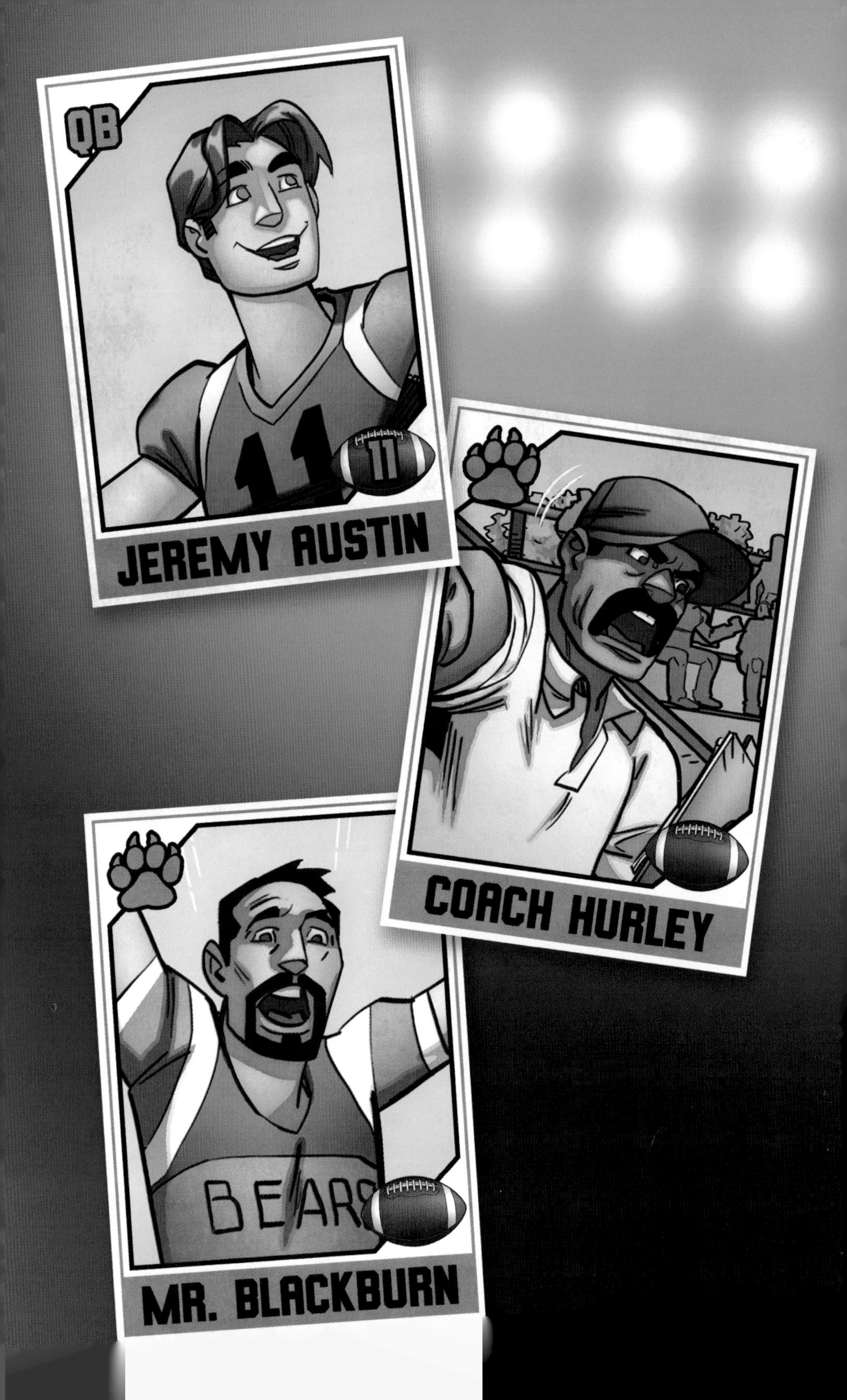
QB
11
JEREMY AUSTIN
COACH HURLEY
MR. BLACKBURN

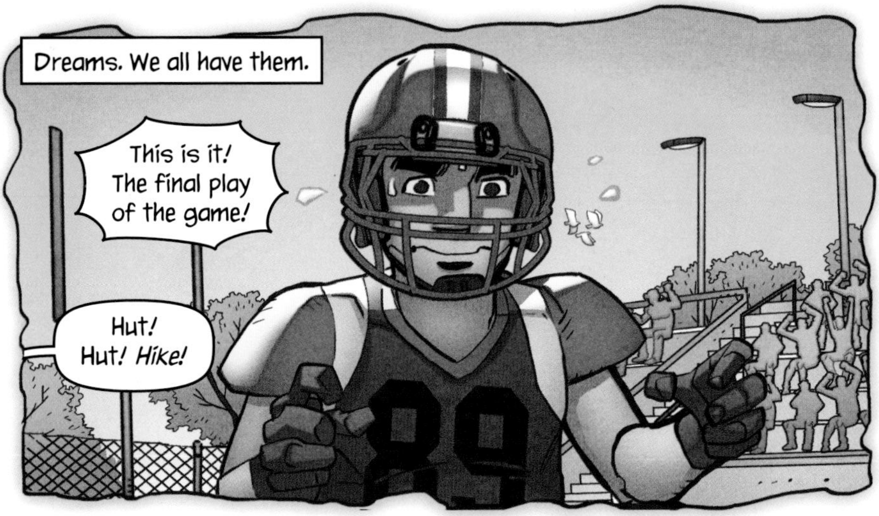
Dreams. We all have them.
This is it! The final play of the game!
Hut! Hut! *Hike!*

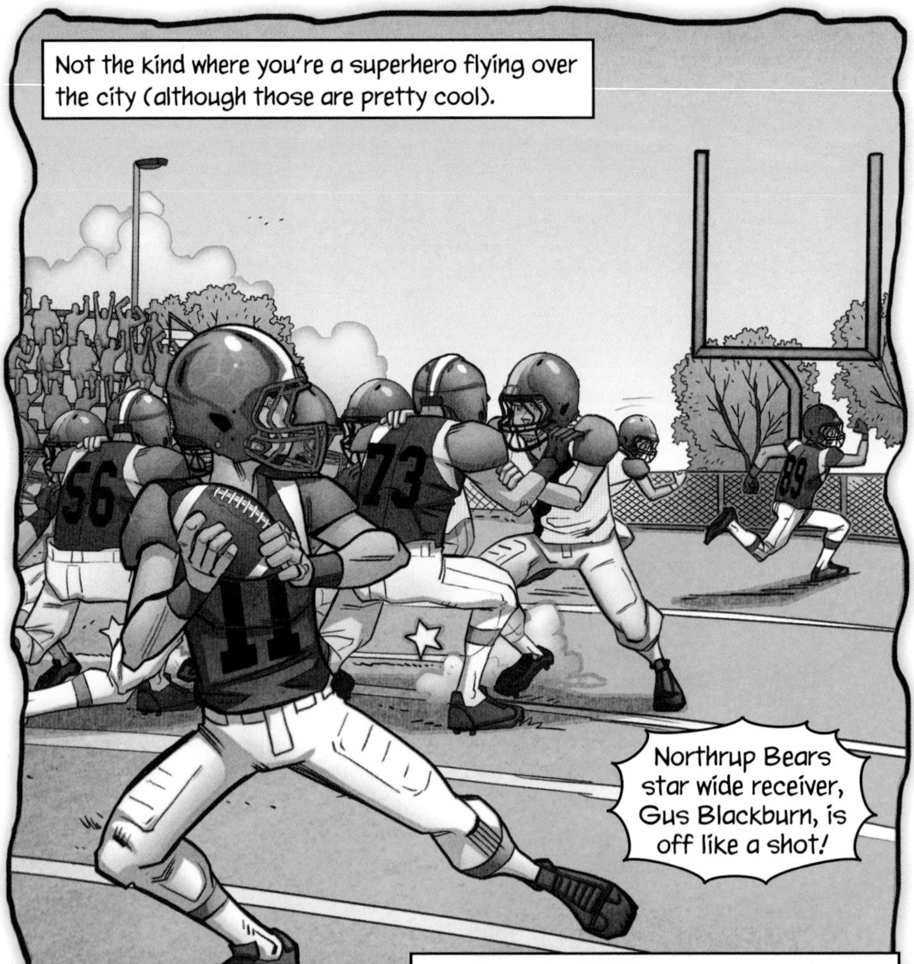
Not the kind where you're a superhero flying over the city (although those are pretty cool).
Northrup Bears star wide receiver, Gus Blackburn, is off like a shot!
Or the kind where you show up at school in your underwear (those are . . . not so cool).

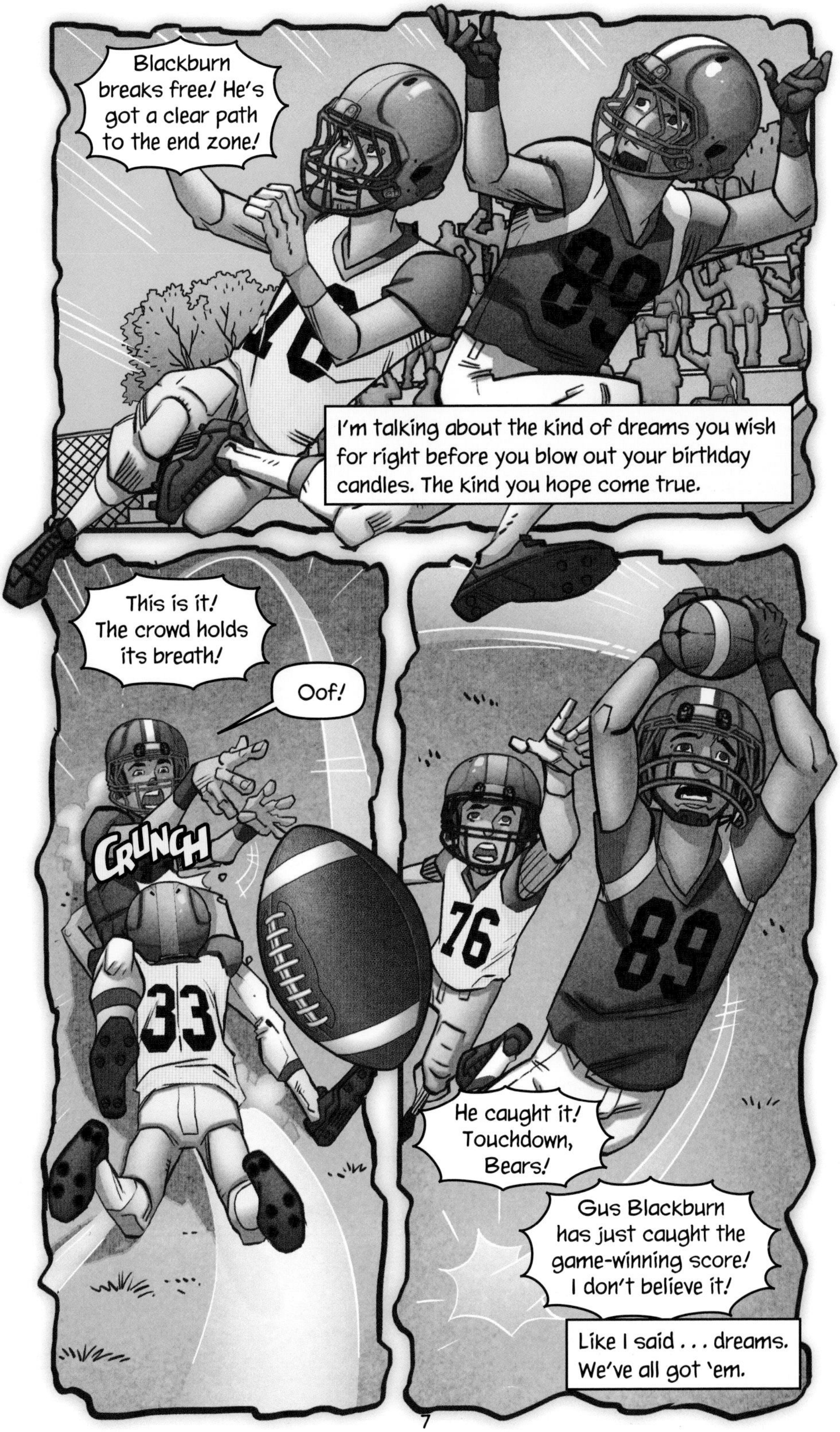
Blackburn breaks free! He's got a clear path to the end zone!
I'm talking about the kind of dreams you wish for right before you blow out your birthday candles. The kind you hope come true.
This is it! The crowd holds its breath!
Oof!
CRUNCH
76
89
33
He caught it! Touchdown, Bears!
Gus Blackburn has just caught the game-winning score! I don't believe it!
Like I said . . . dreams. We've all got 'em.

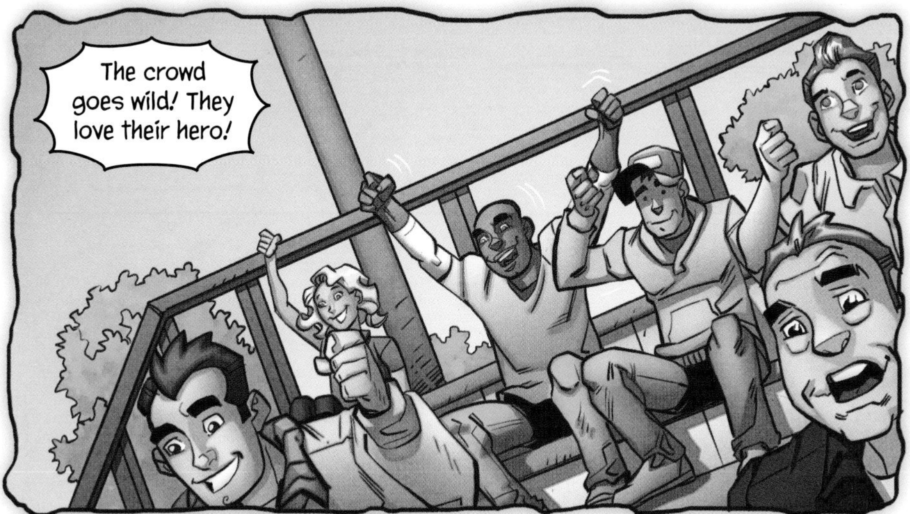
The crowd goes wild! They love their hero!

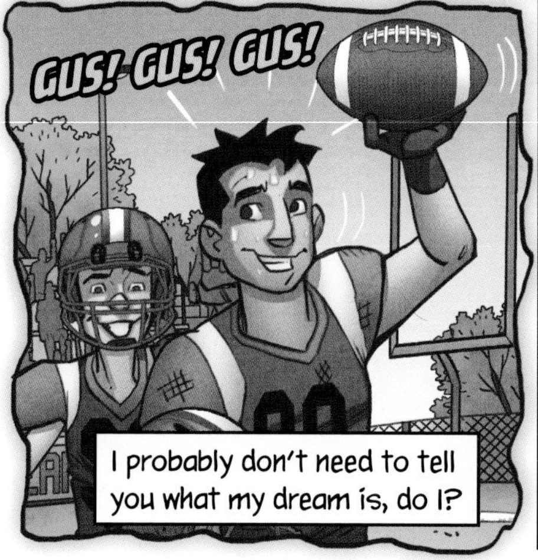
GUS! GUS! GUS!
I probably don't need to tell you what my dream is, do I?

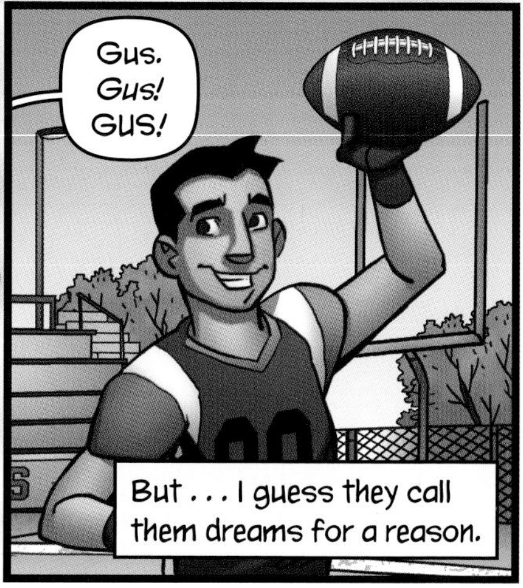
Gus. Gus! GUS!
But . . . I guess they call them dreams for a reason.

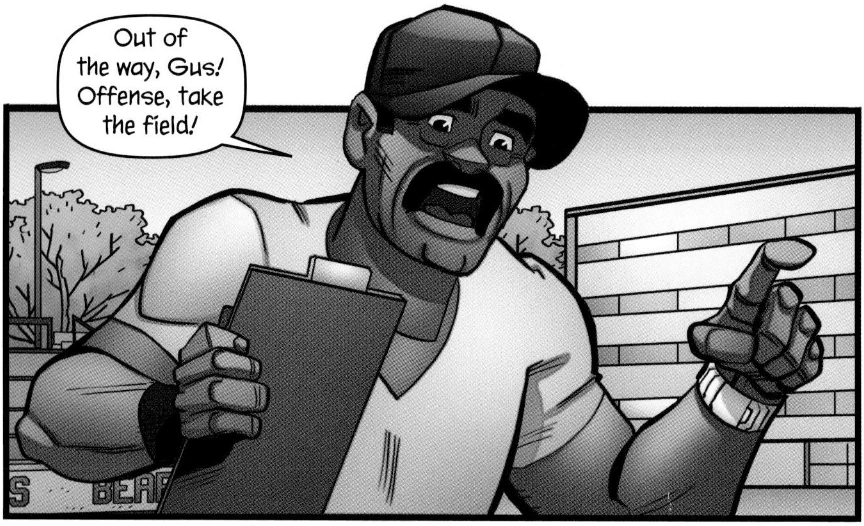
Out of the way, Gus! Offense, take the field!

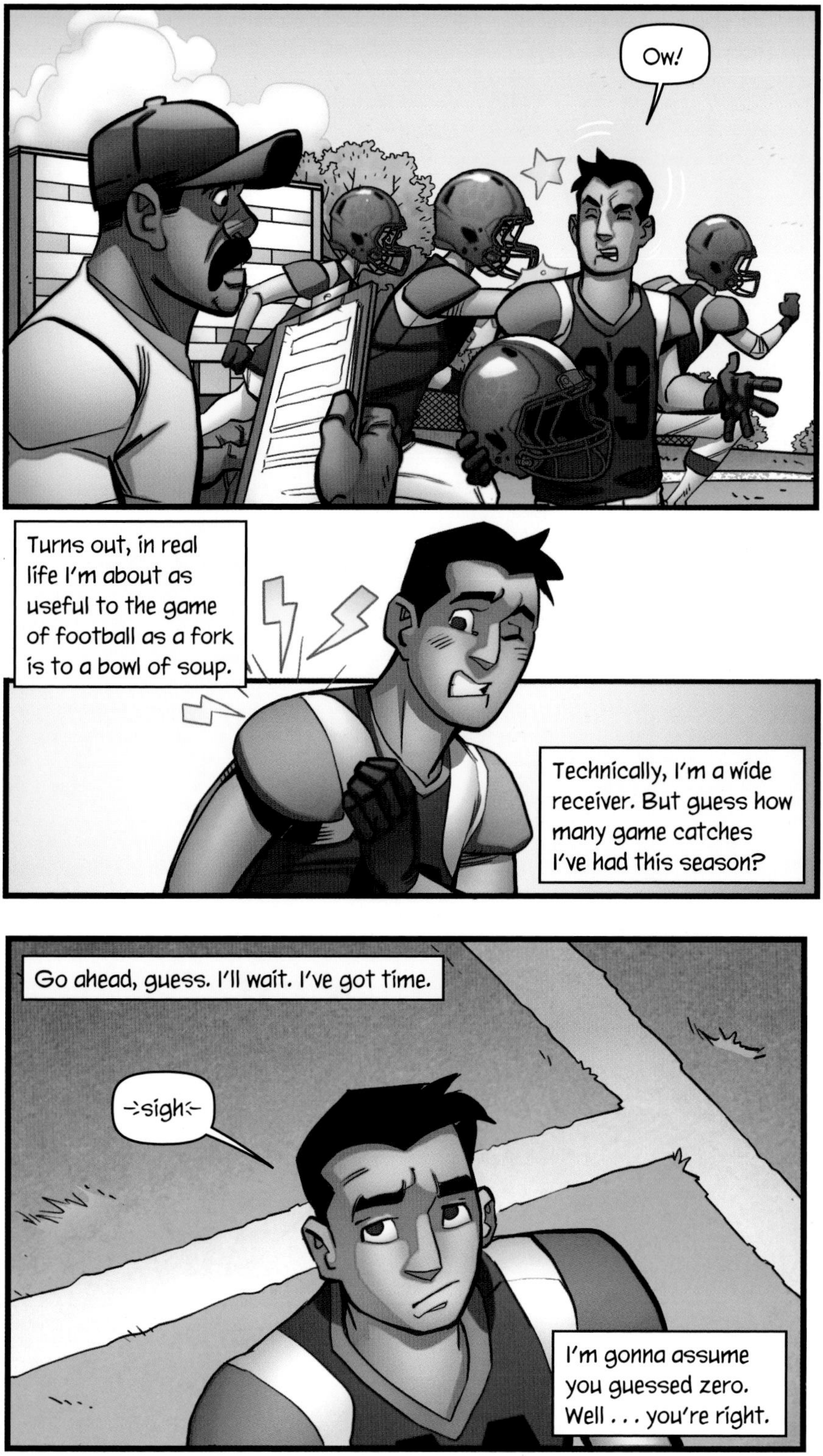
Ow!
Turns out, in real life I'm about as useful to the game of football as a fork is to a bowl of soup.
Technically, I'm a wide receiver. But guess how many game catches I've had this season?
Go ahead, guess. I'll wait. I've got time.
-sigh-
I'm gonna assume you guessed zero. Well . . . you're right.

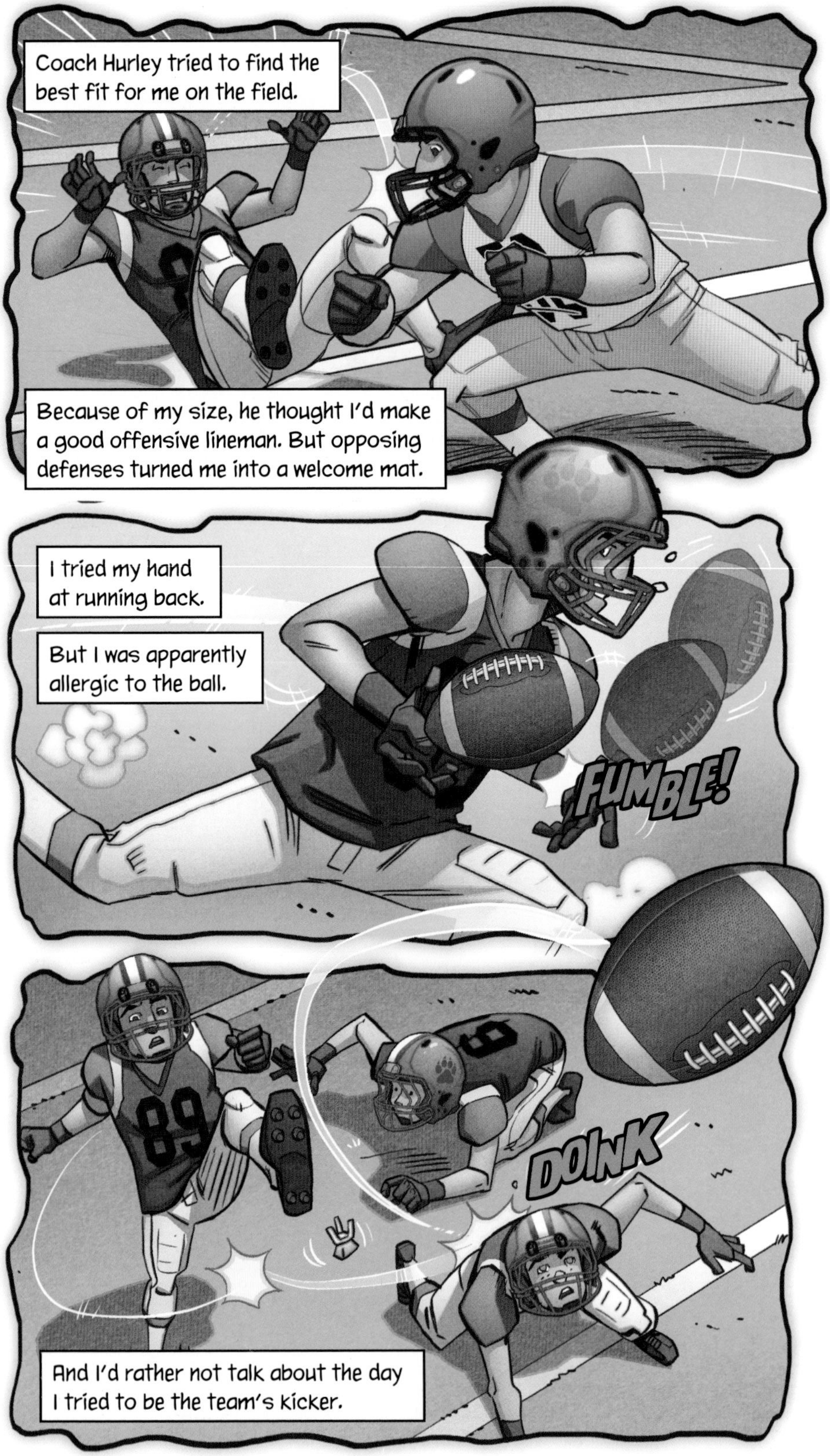
Coach Hurley tried to find the best fit for me on the field.
Because of my size, he thought I'd make a good offensive lineman. But opposing defenses turned me into a welcome mat.
I tried my hand at running back.
But I was apparently allergic to the ball.
FUMBLE!
DOINK
And I'd rather not talk about the day I tried to be the team's kicker.

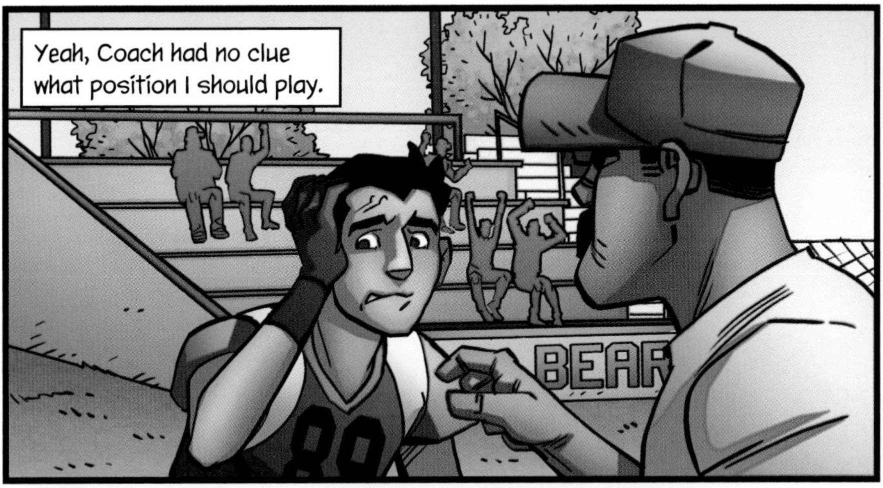
Yeah, Coach had no clue what position I should play.
BEAR

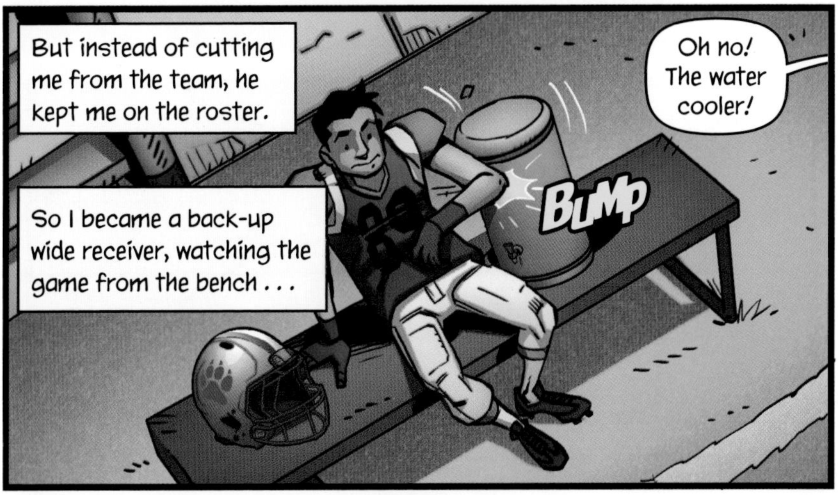
But instead of cutting me from the team, he kept me on the roster.
Oh no! The water cooler!
So I became a back-up wide receiver, watching the game from the bench . . .
BUMP

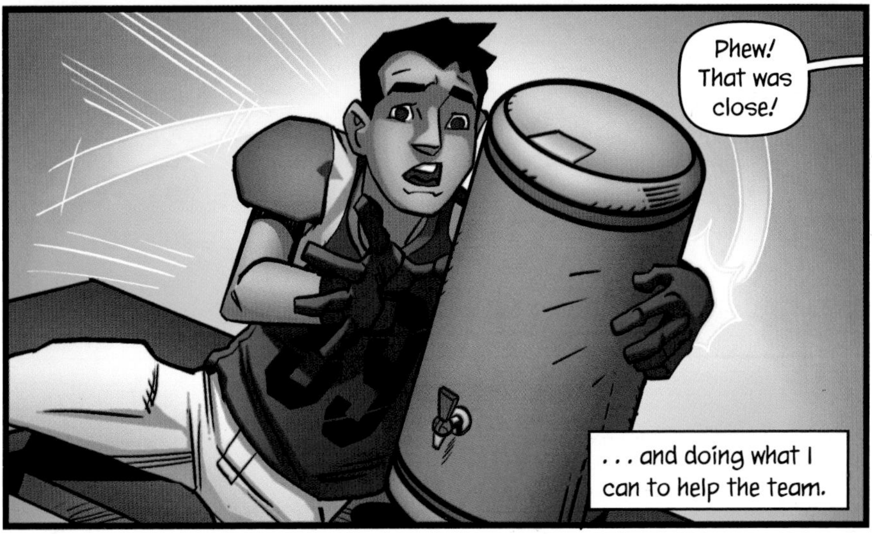
Phew! That was close!
. . . and doing what I can to help the team.

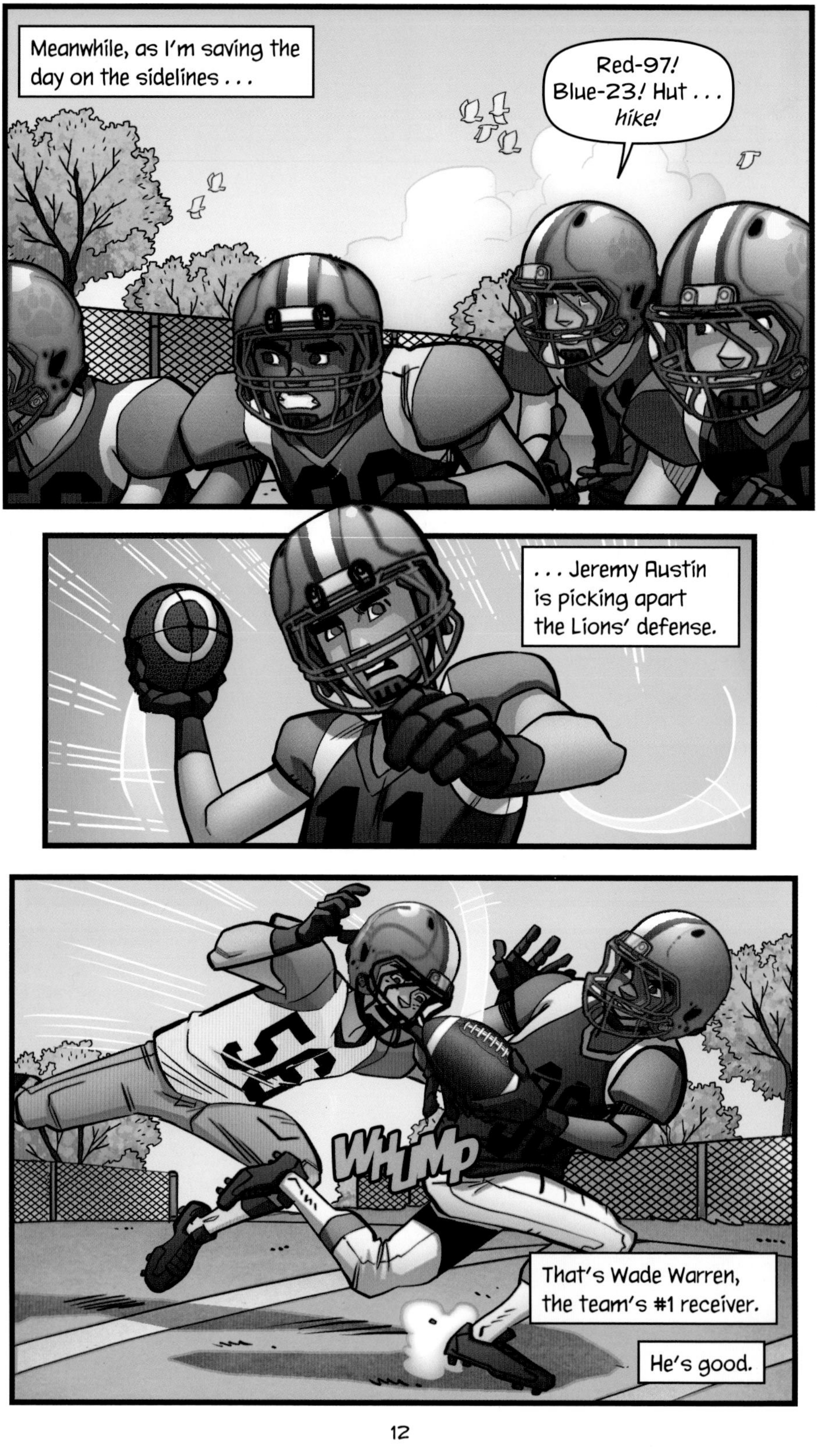
Meanwhile, as I'm saving the day on the sidelines . . .
Red-97! Blue-23! Hut . . . *hike!*
. . . Jeremy Austin is picking apart the Lions' defense.
WHUMP
That's Wade Warren, the team's #1 receiver.
He's good.

13

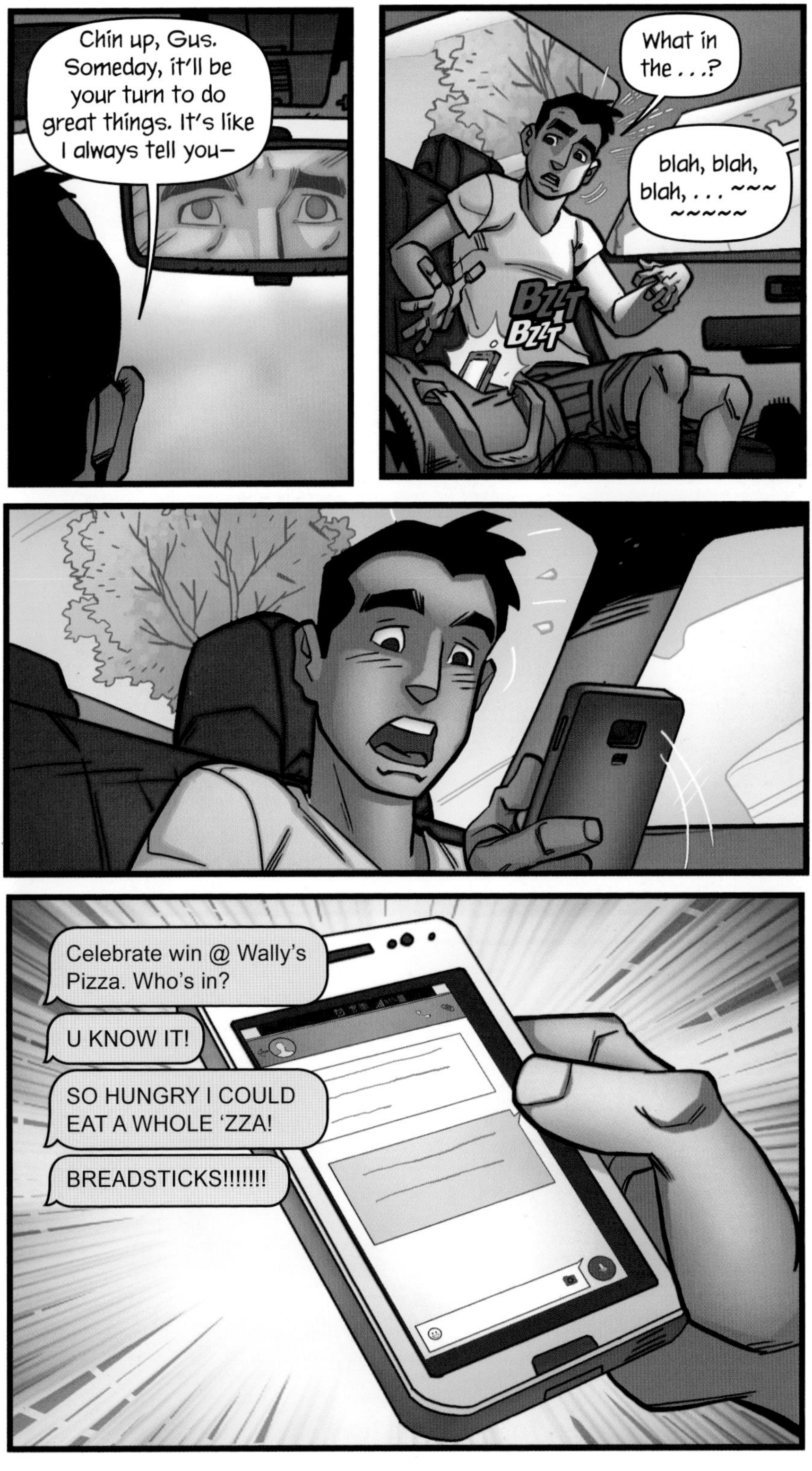
Chin up, Gus. Someday, it'll be your turn to do great things. It's like I always tell you—
What in the . . .?
blah, blah, blah, . . . ~~~ ~~~~~
BZZT
BZZT
Celebrate win @ Wally's Pizza. Who's in?
U KNOW IT!
SO HUNGRY I COULD EAT A WHOLE 'ZZA!
BREADSTICKS!!!!!!!

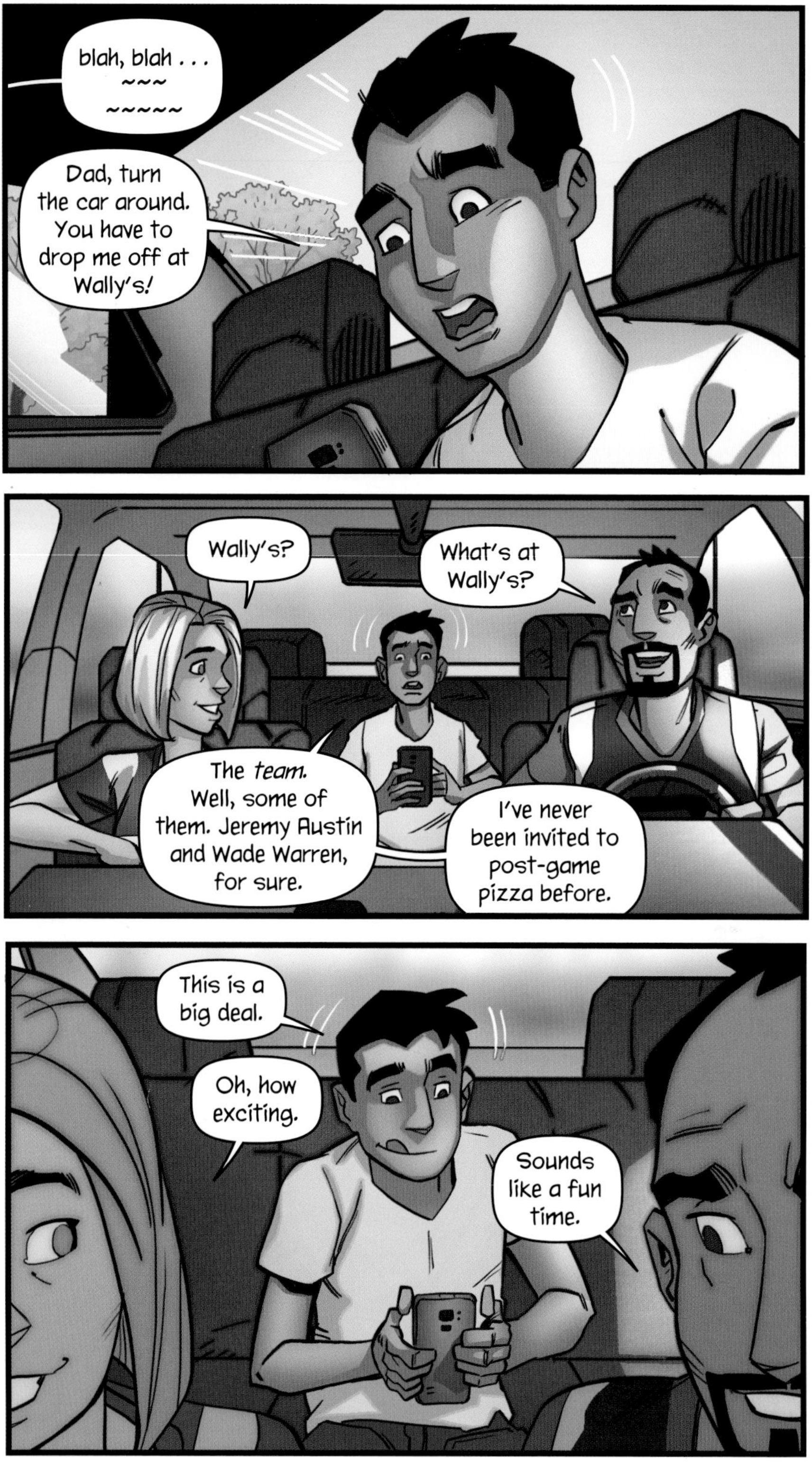
blah, blah . . .
~~~
~~~~~
Dad, turn the car around. You have to drop me off at Wally's!
Wally's?
What's at Wally's?
The *team.* Well, some of them. Jeremy Austin and Wade Warren, for sure.
I've never been invited to post-game pizza before.
This is a big deal.
Oh, how exciting.
Sounds like a fun time.

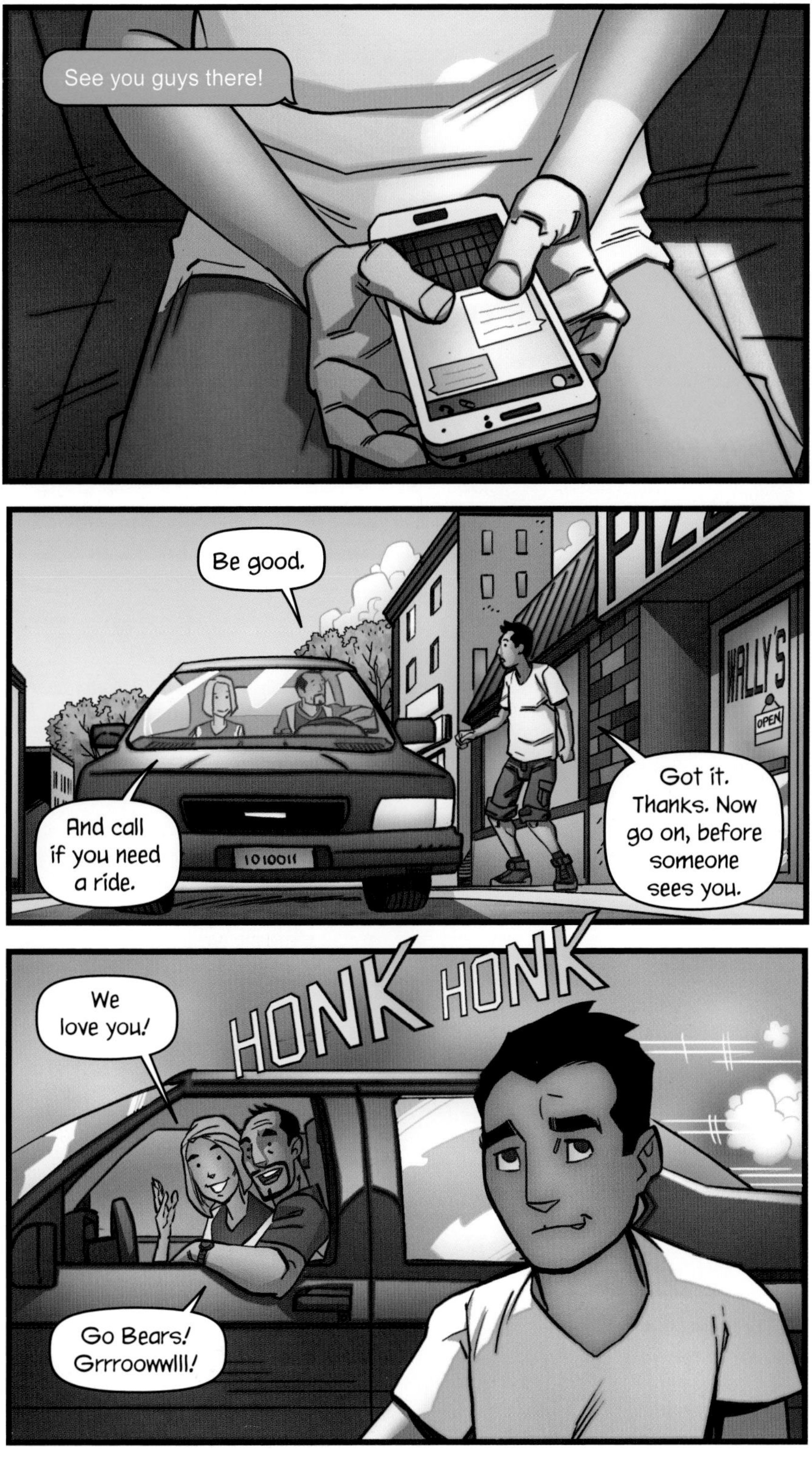
See you guys there!
Be good.
And call if you need a ride.
Got it. Thanks. Now go on, before someone sees you.
PIZ
WALLY'S
OPEN
1010011
HONK HONK
We love you!
Go Bears! Grrroowwlll!

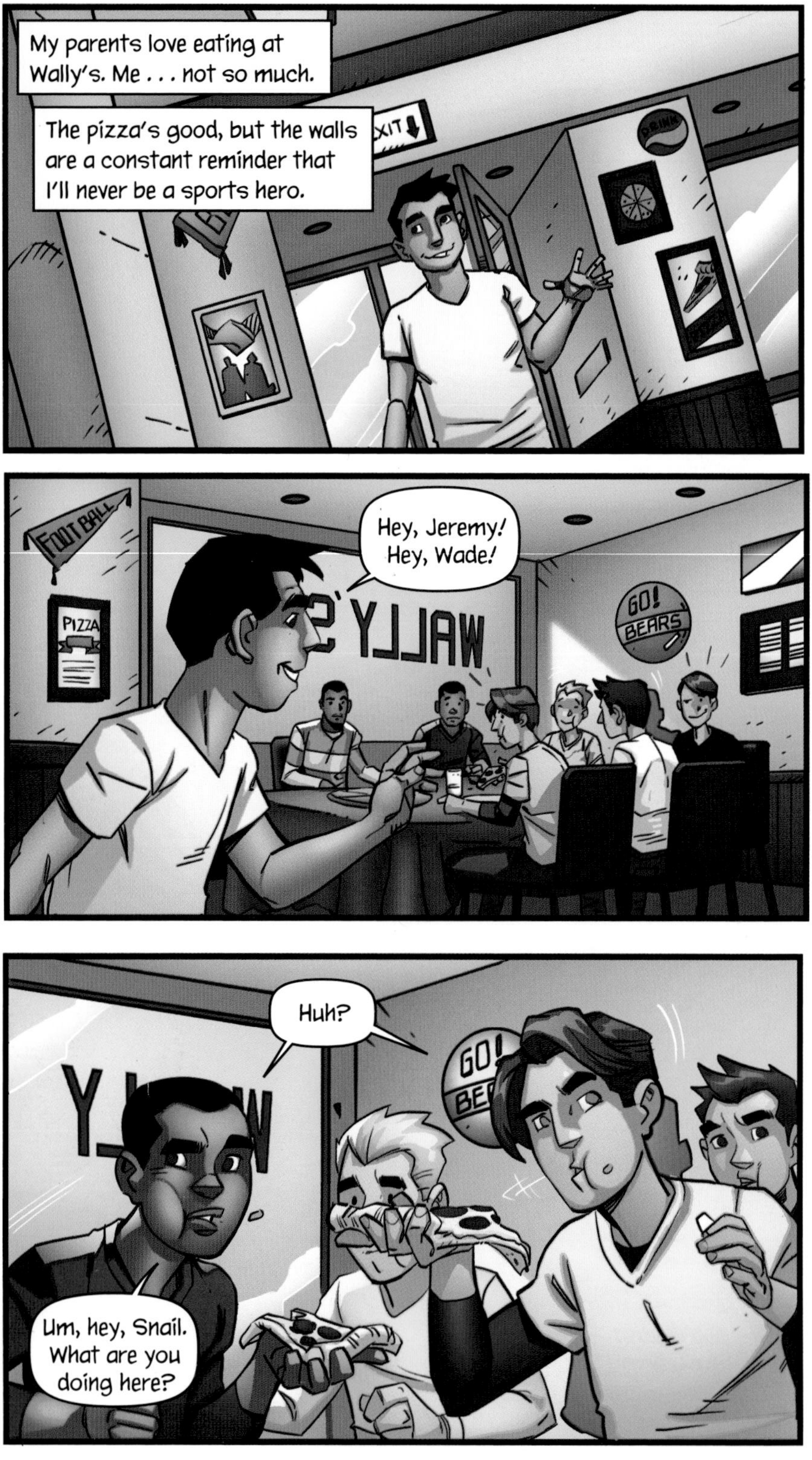
My parents love eating at Wally's. Me . . . not so much.
The pizza's good, but the walls are a constant reminder that I'll never be a sports hero.
Hey, Jeremy! Hey, Wade!
FOOTBALL
PIZZA
GO! BEARS
Huh?
Um, hey, Snail. What are you doing here?

19

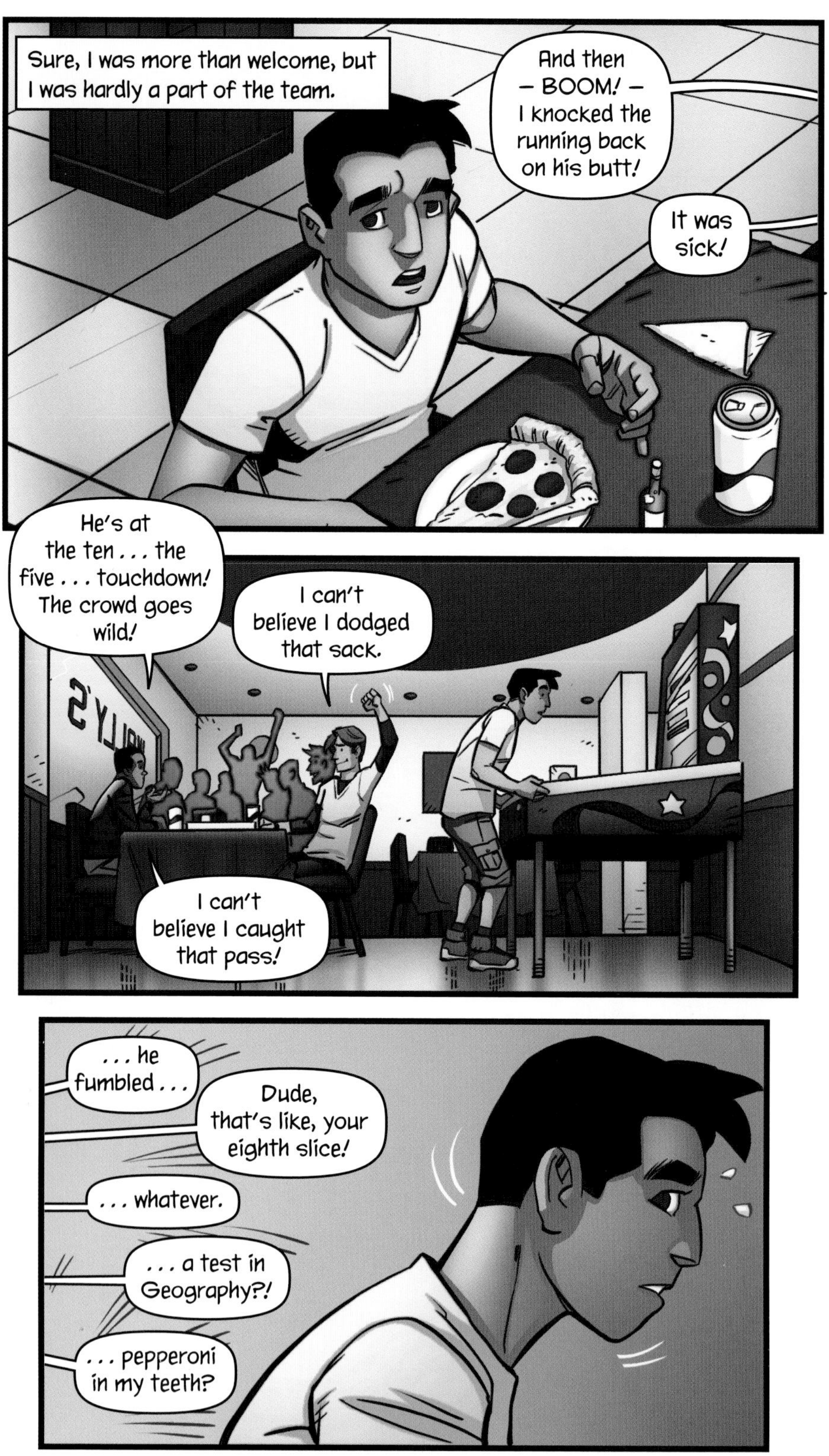
Sure, I was more than welcome, but I was hardly a part of the team.
And then — BOOM! — I knocked the running back on his butt!
It was sick!
He's at the ten . . . the five . . . touchdown! The crowd goes wild!
I can't believe I dodged that sack.
WALLY'S
I can't believe I caught that pass!
. . . he fumbled . . .
Dude, that's like, your eighth slice!
. . . whatever.
. . . a test in Geography?!
. . . pepperoni in my teeth?

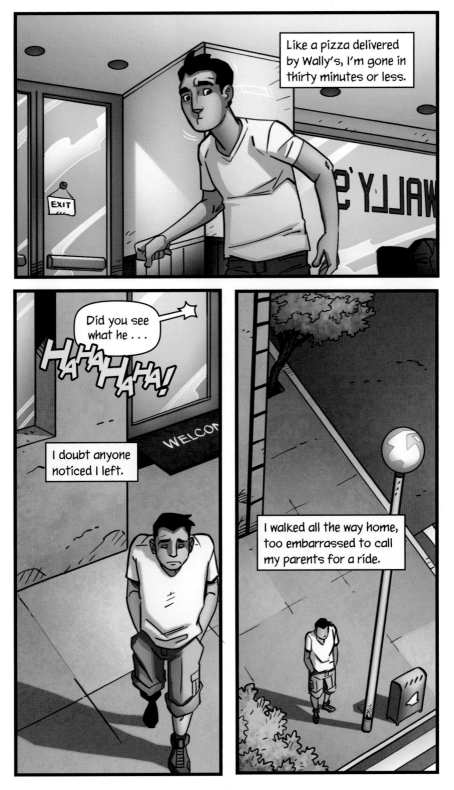

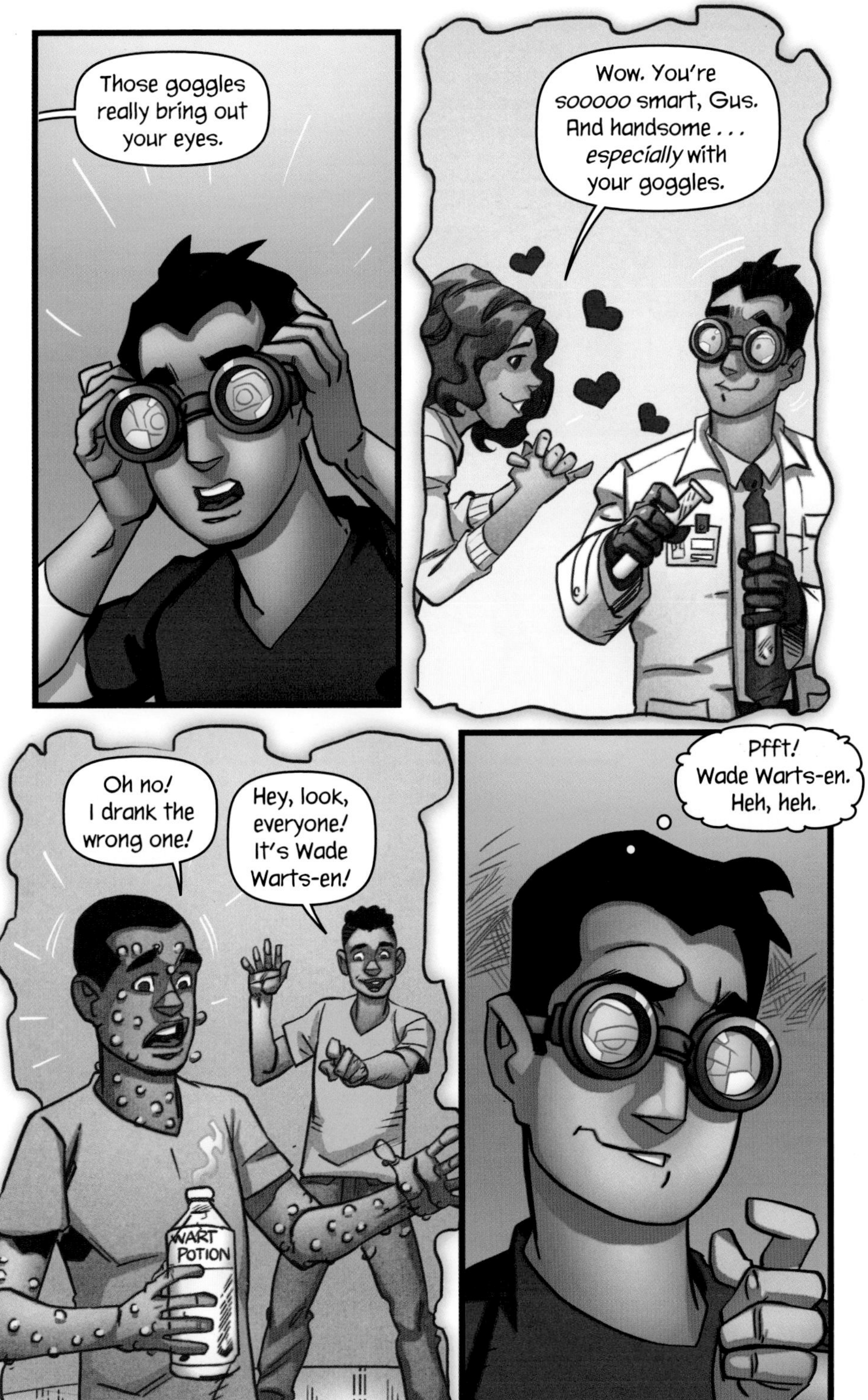
Those goggles really bring out your eyes.
Wow. You're *sooooo* smart, Gus. And handsome . . . *especially* with your goggles.
Oh no! I drank the wrong one!
Hey, look, everyone! It's Wade Warts-en!
WART POTION
Pfft! Wade Warts-en. Heh, heh.

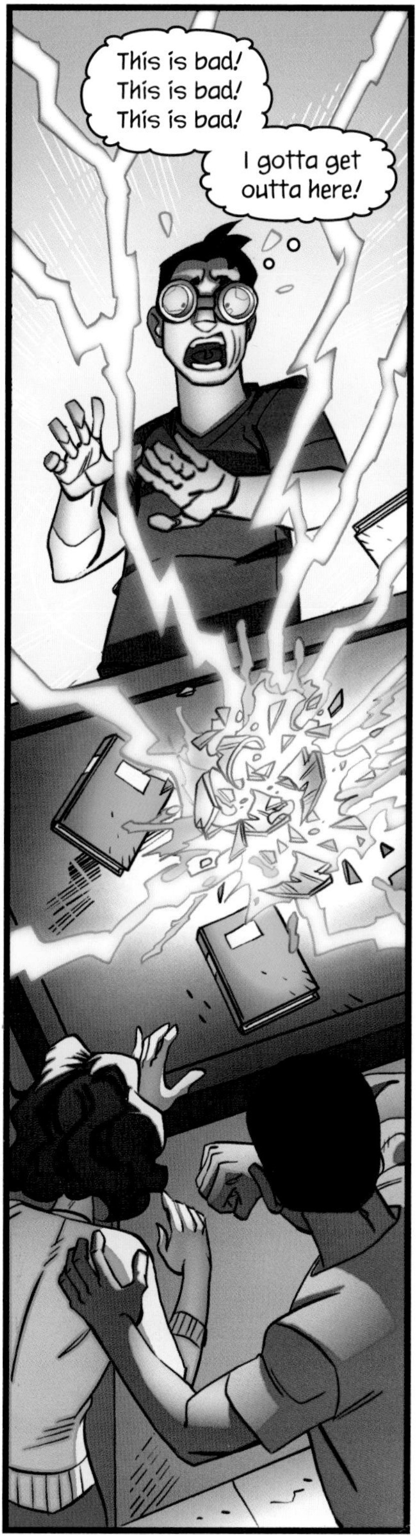
This is bad! This is bad! This is bad!
I gotta get outta here!

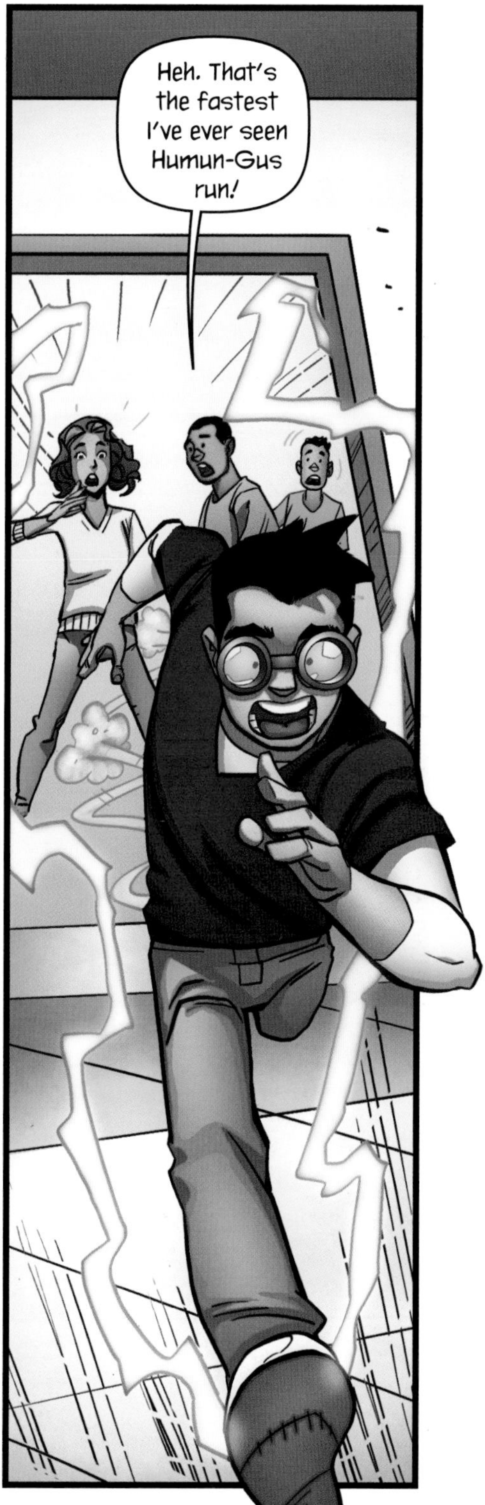
Heh. That's the fastest I've ever seen Humun-Gus run!

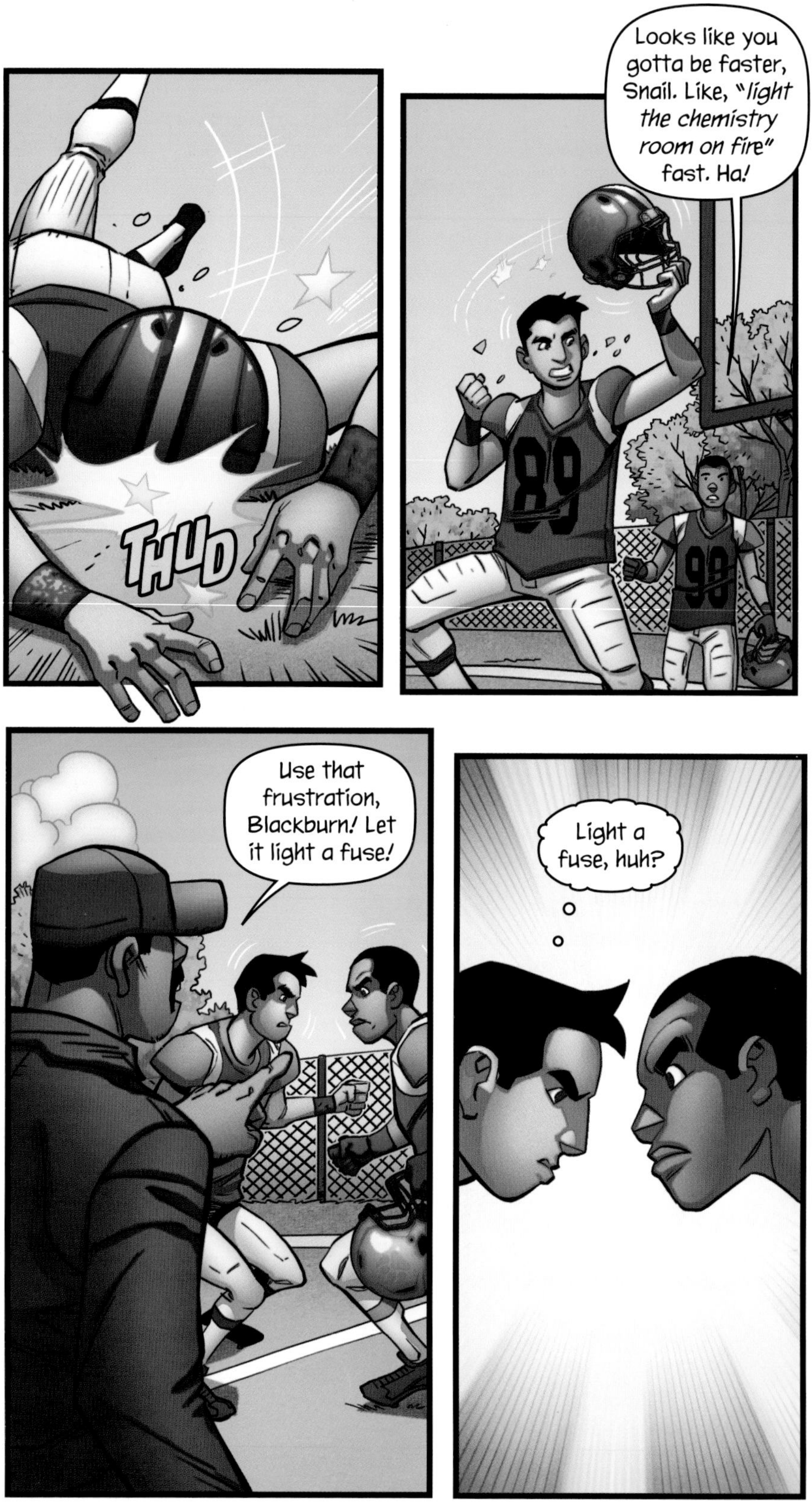
THUD
Looks like you gotta be faster, Snail. Like, "light the chemistry room on fire" fast. Ha!
Use that frustration, Blackburn! Let it light a fuse!
Light a fuse, huh?

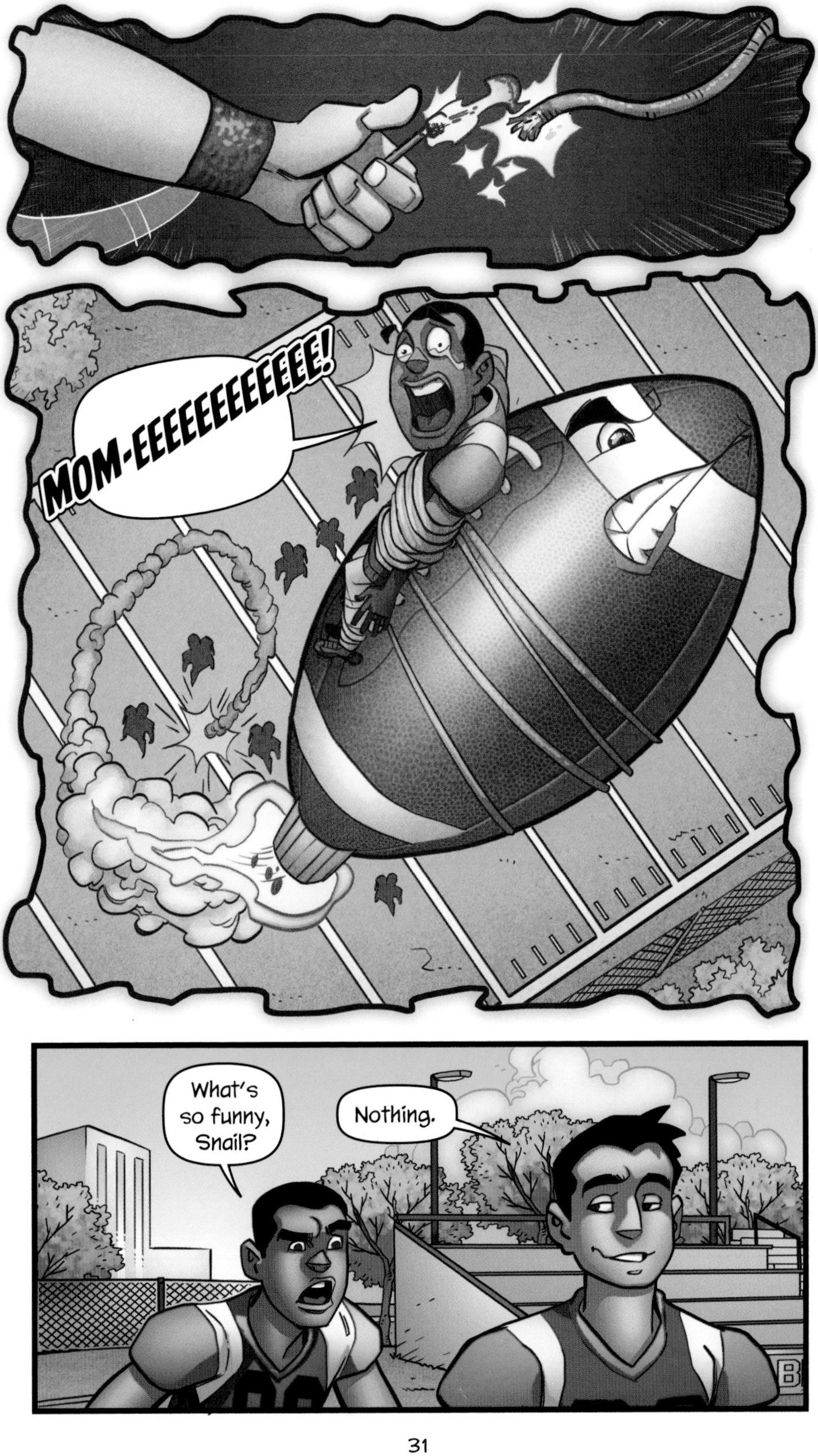
MOM-EEEEEEEEEEEE!
What's so funny, Snail?
Nothing.

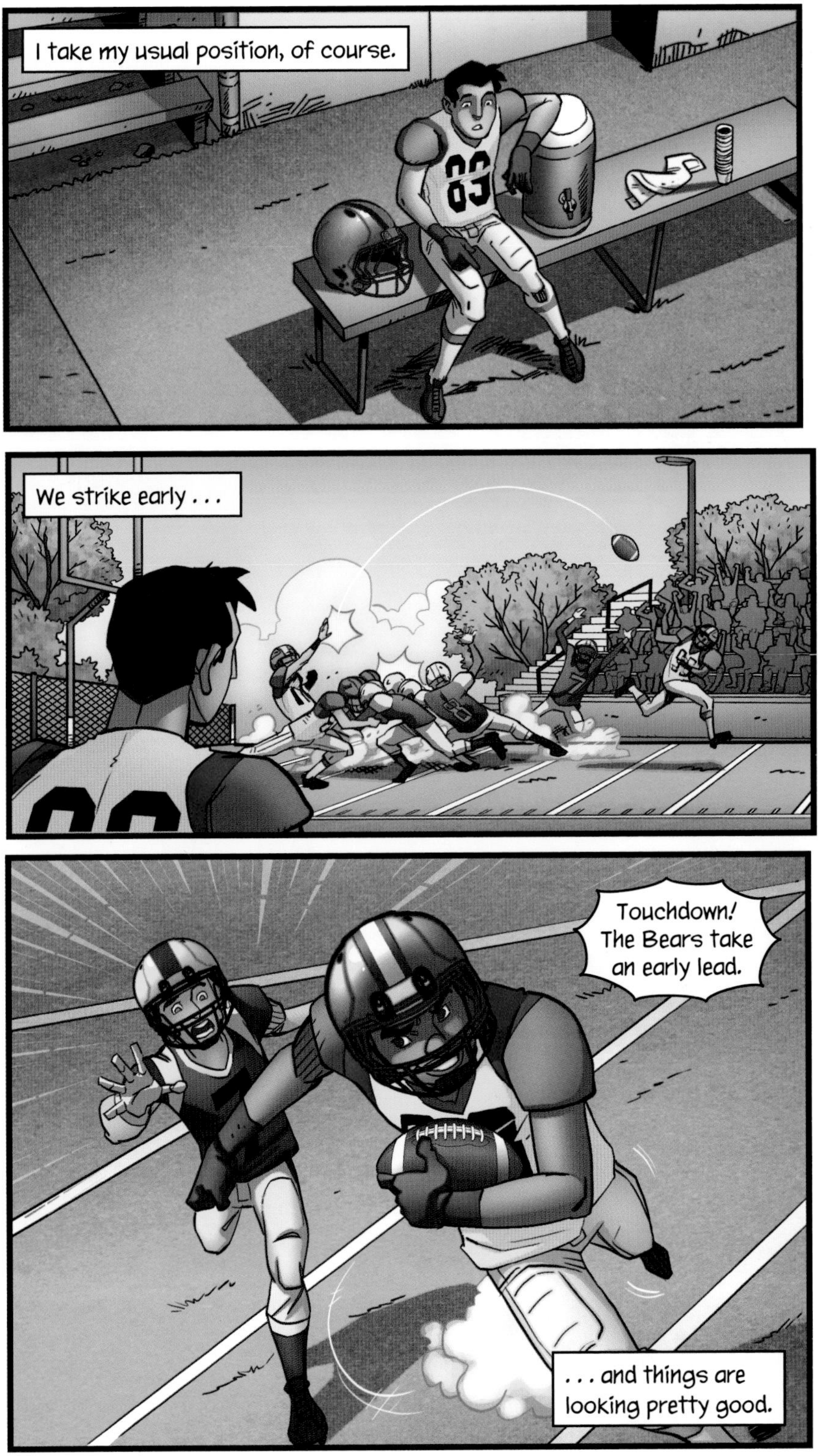
I take my usual position, of course.
We strike early . . .
Touchdown! The Bears take an early lead.
. . . and things are looking pretty good.

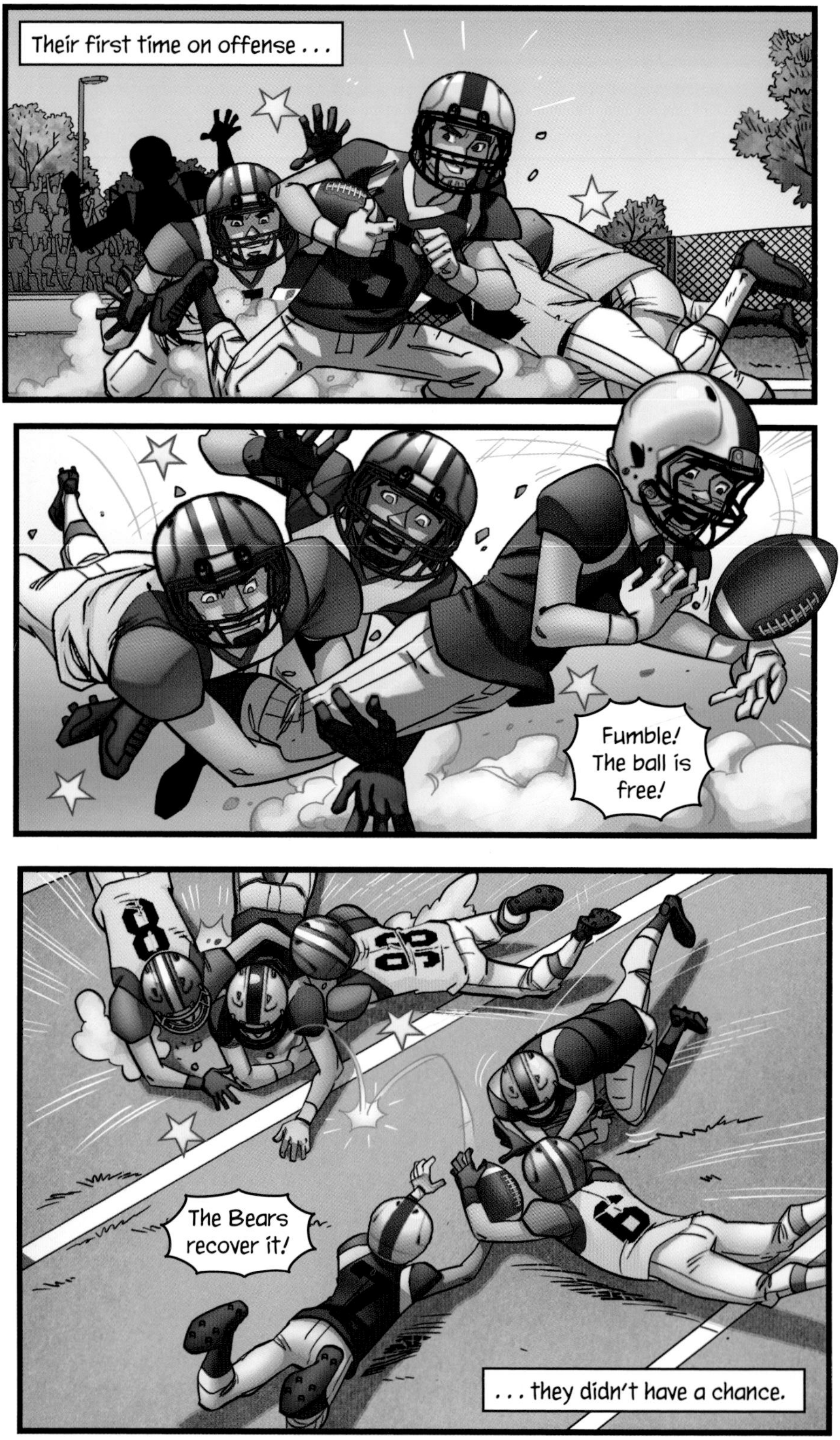
Their first time on offense . . .
Fumble! The ball is free!
The Bears recover it!
. . . they didn't have a chance.

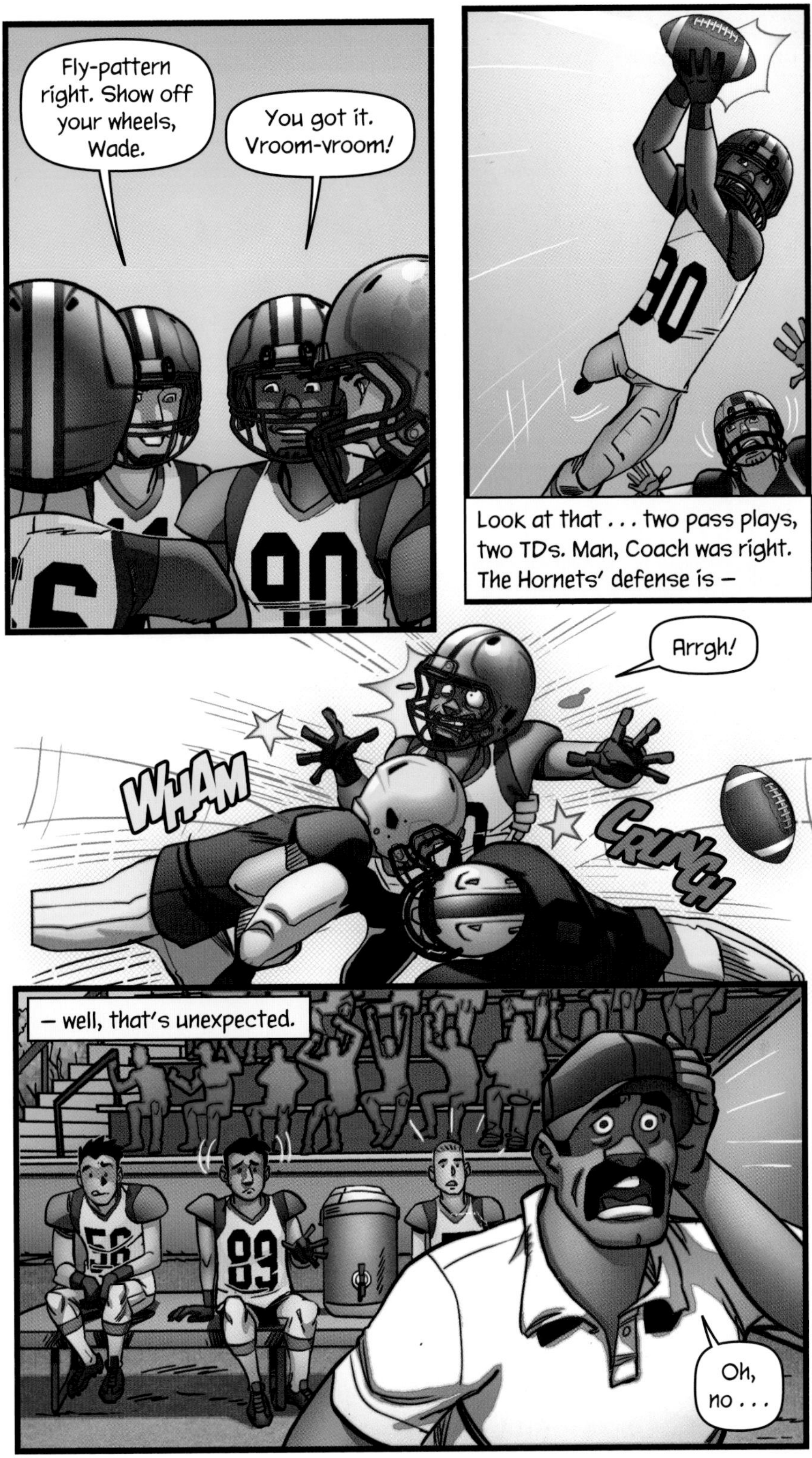
Fly-pattern right. Show off your wheels, Wade.
You got it. Vroom-vroom!
Look at that . . . two pass plays, two TDs. Man, Coach was right. The Hornets' defense is —
Arrgh!
WHAM
CRUNCH
— well, that's unexpected.
Oh, no . . .

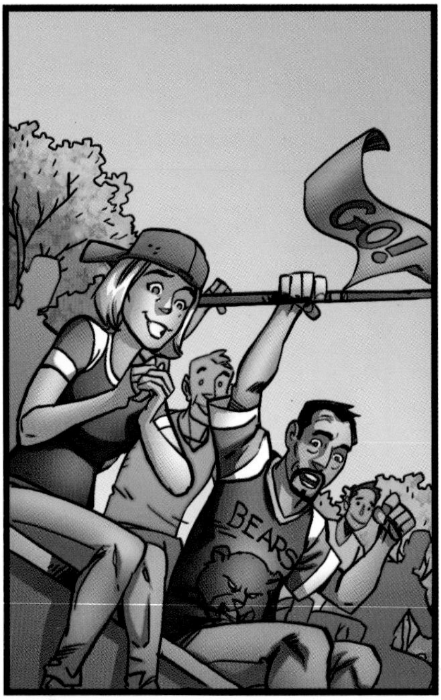
GO!
BEARS

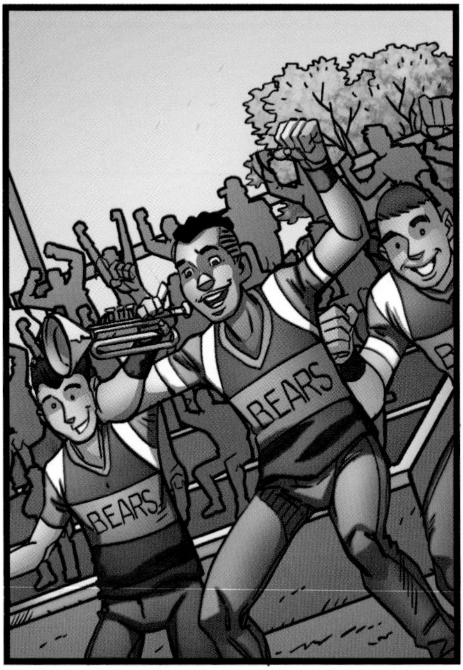
BEARS
BEARS

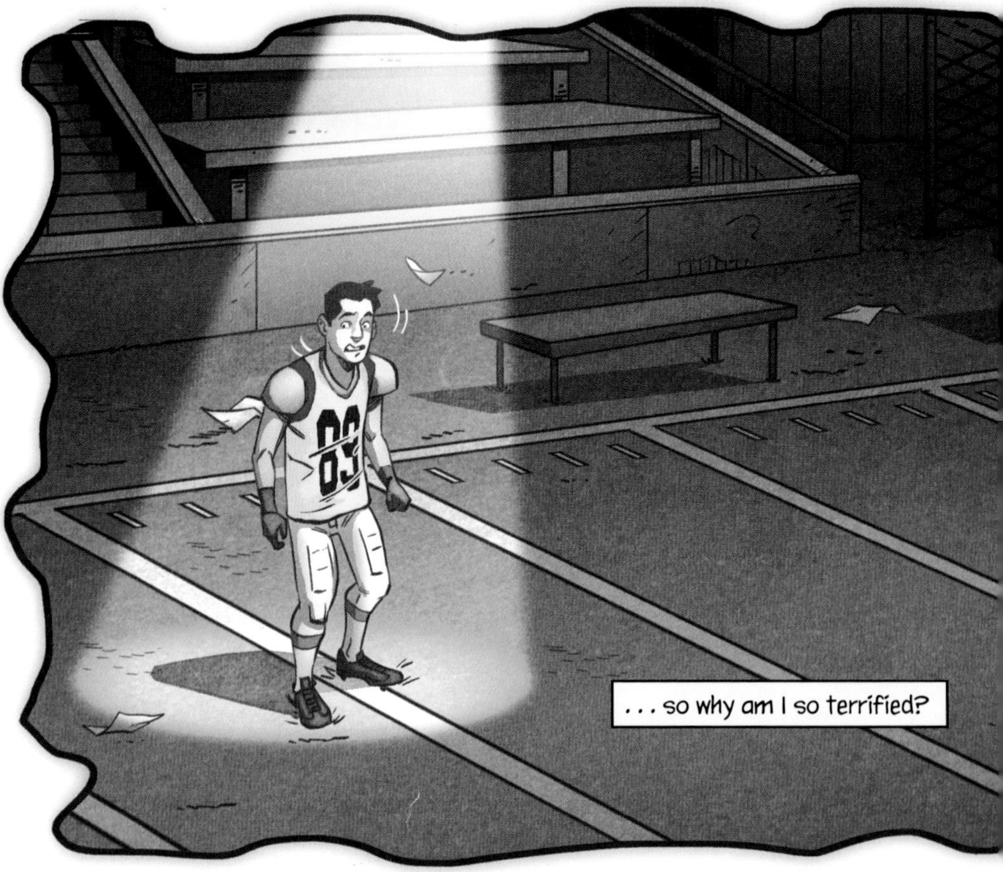
. . . so why am I so terrified?

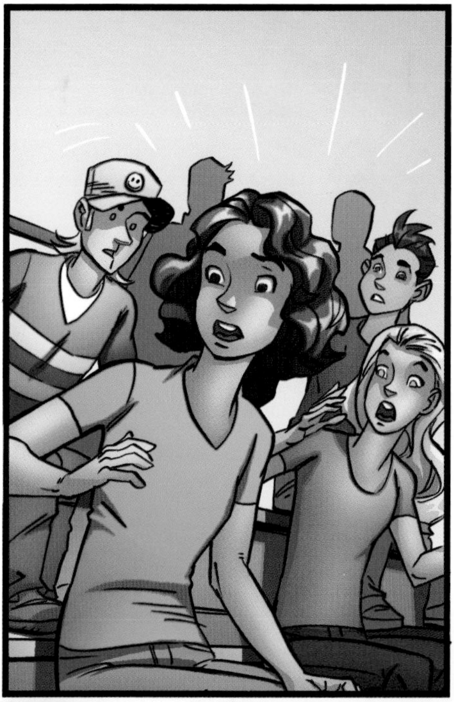

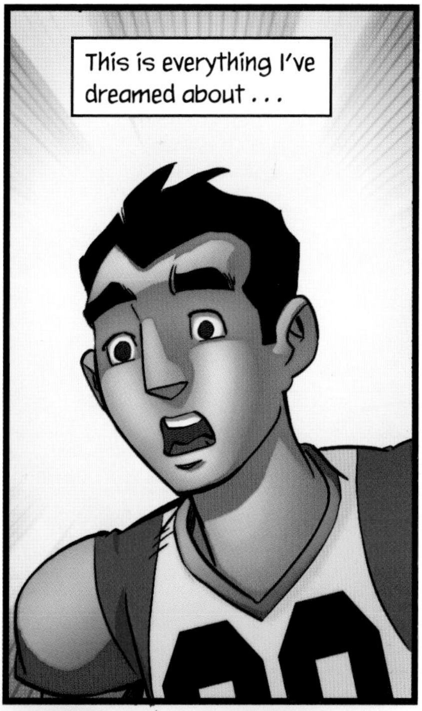
This is everything I've dreamed about . . .

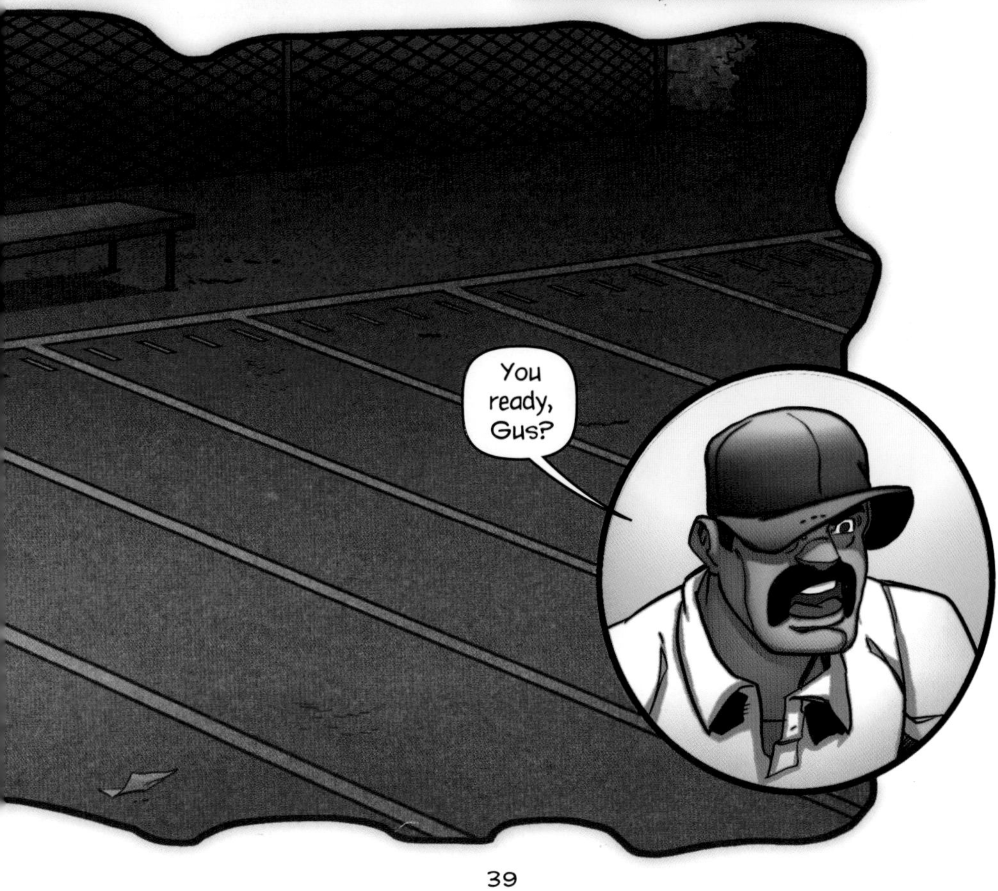
You ready, Gus?

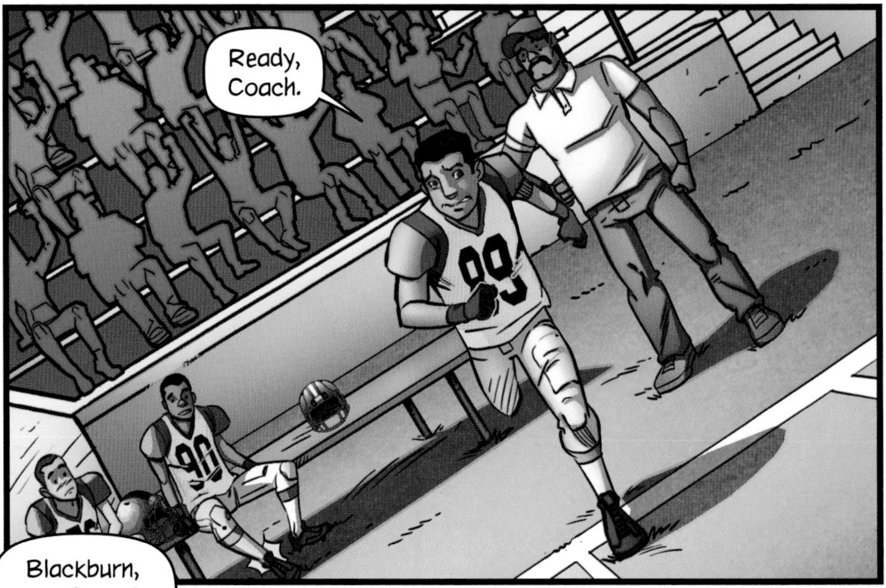
Ready, Coach.

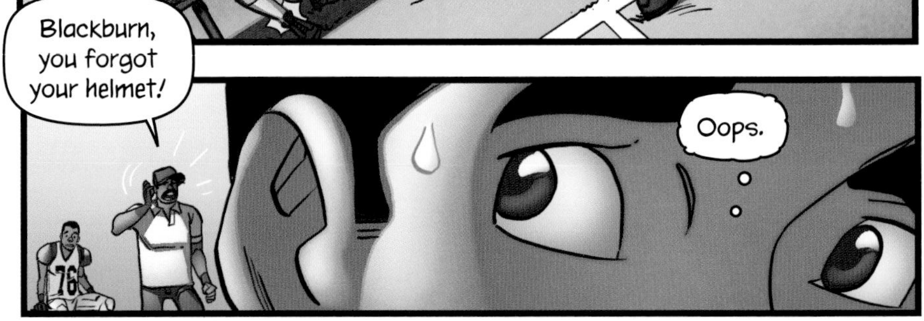
Blackburn, you forgot your helmet!
Oops.

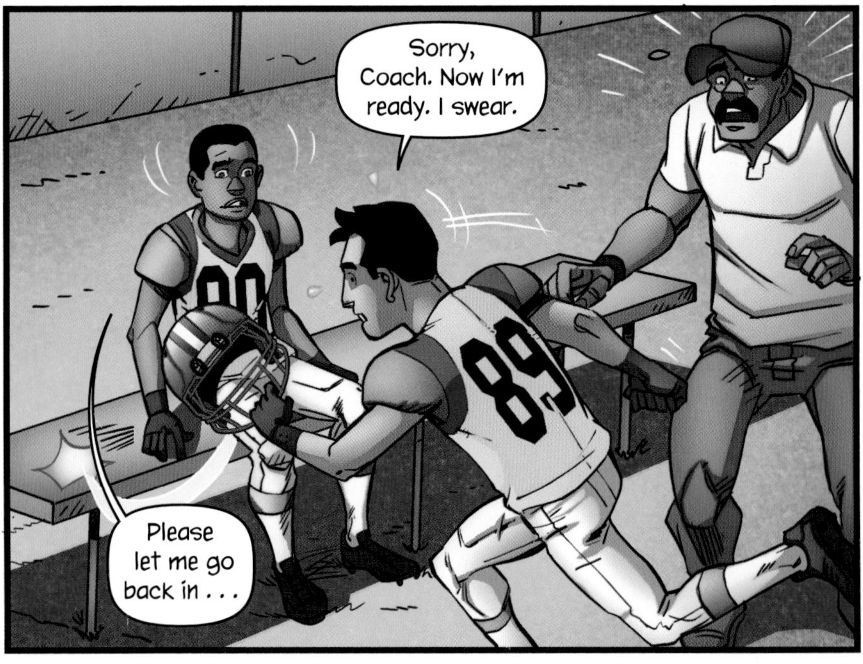
Sorry, Coach. Now I'm ready. I swear.
Please let me go back in . . .

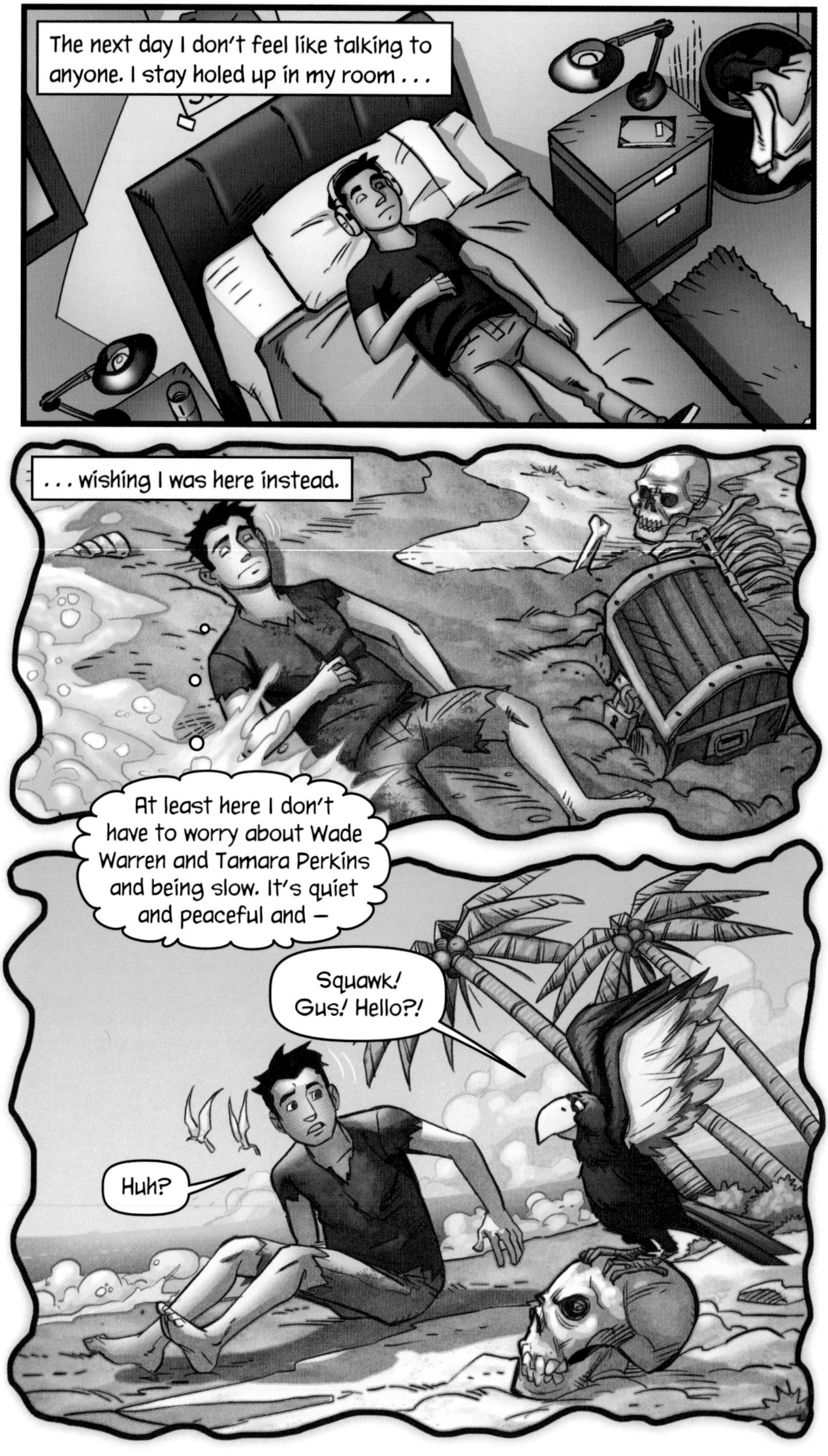
The next day I don't feel like talking to anyone. I stay holed up in my room . . .
. . . wishing I was here instead.
At least here I don't have to worry about Wade Warren and Tamara Perkins and being slow. It's quiet and peaceful and –
Squawk! Gus! Hello?!
Huh?

46

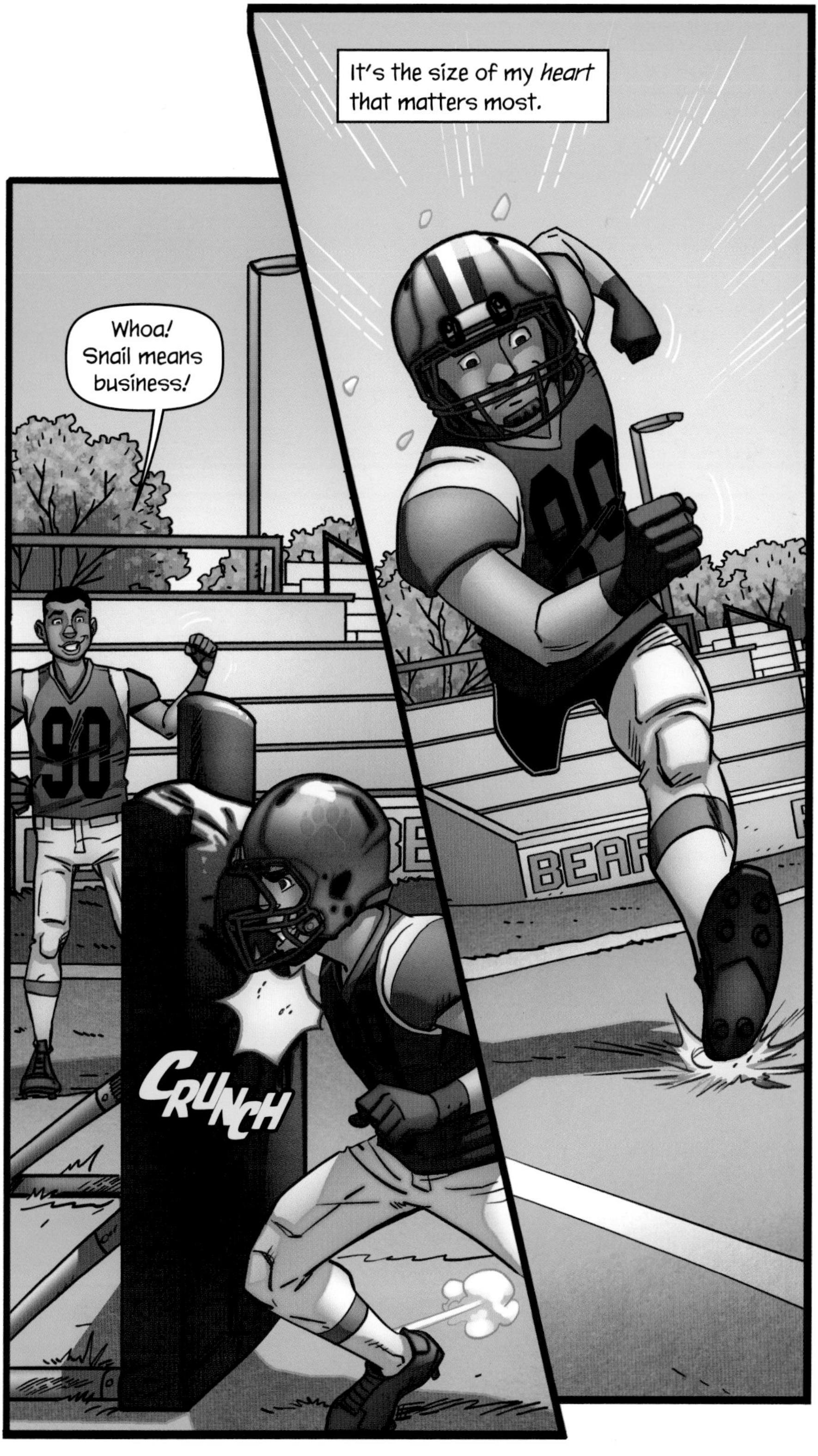
Whoa! Snail means business!
CRUNCH
It's the size of my *heart* that matters most.
BE
BEAR

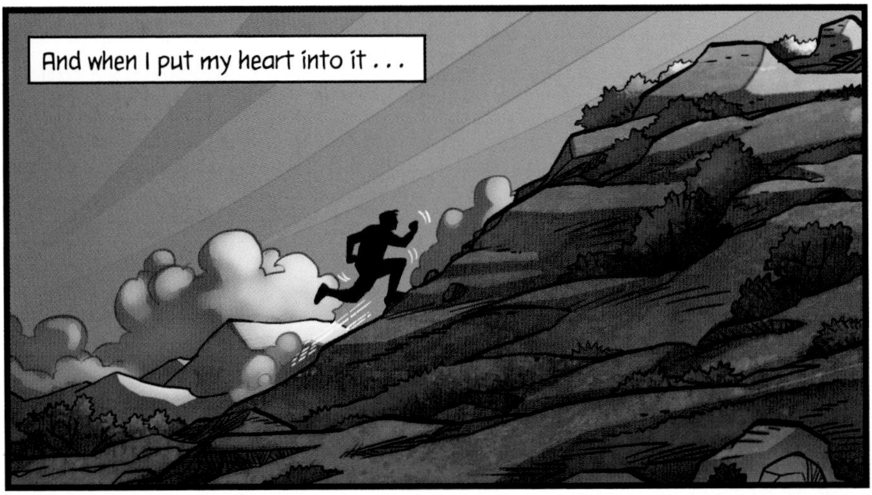
And when I put my heart into it . . .

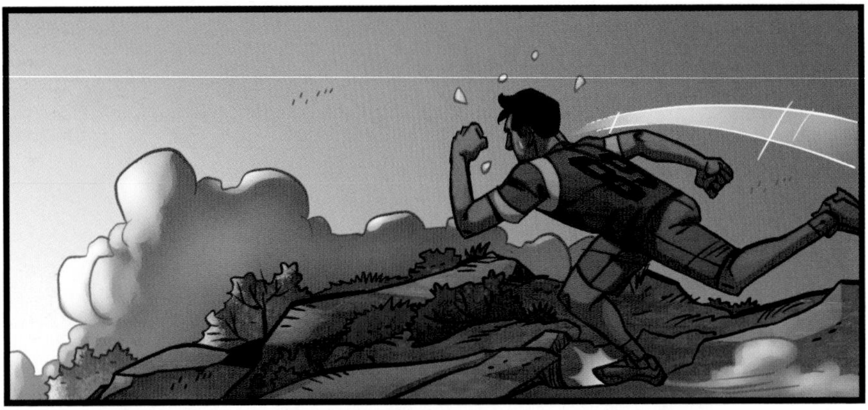

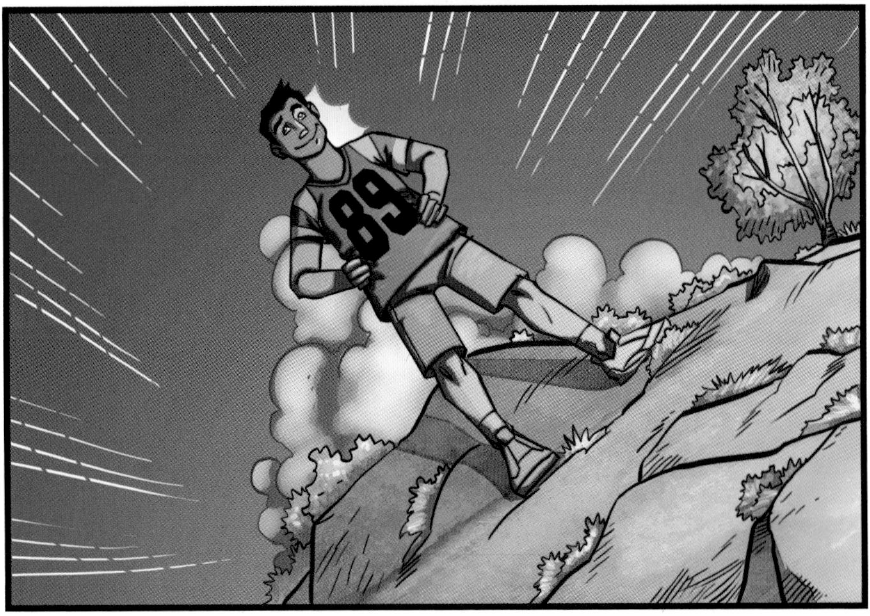
89

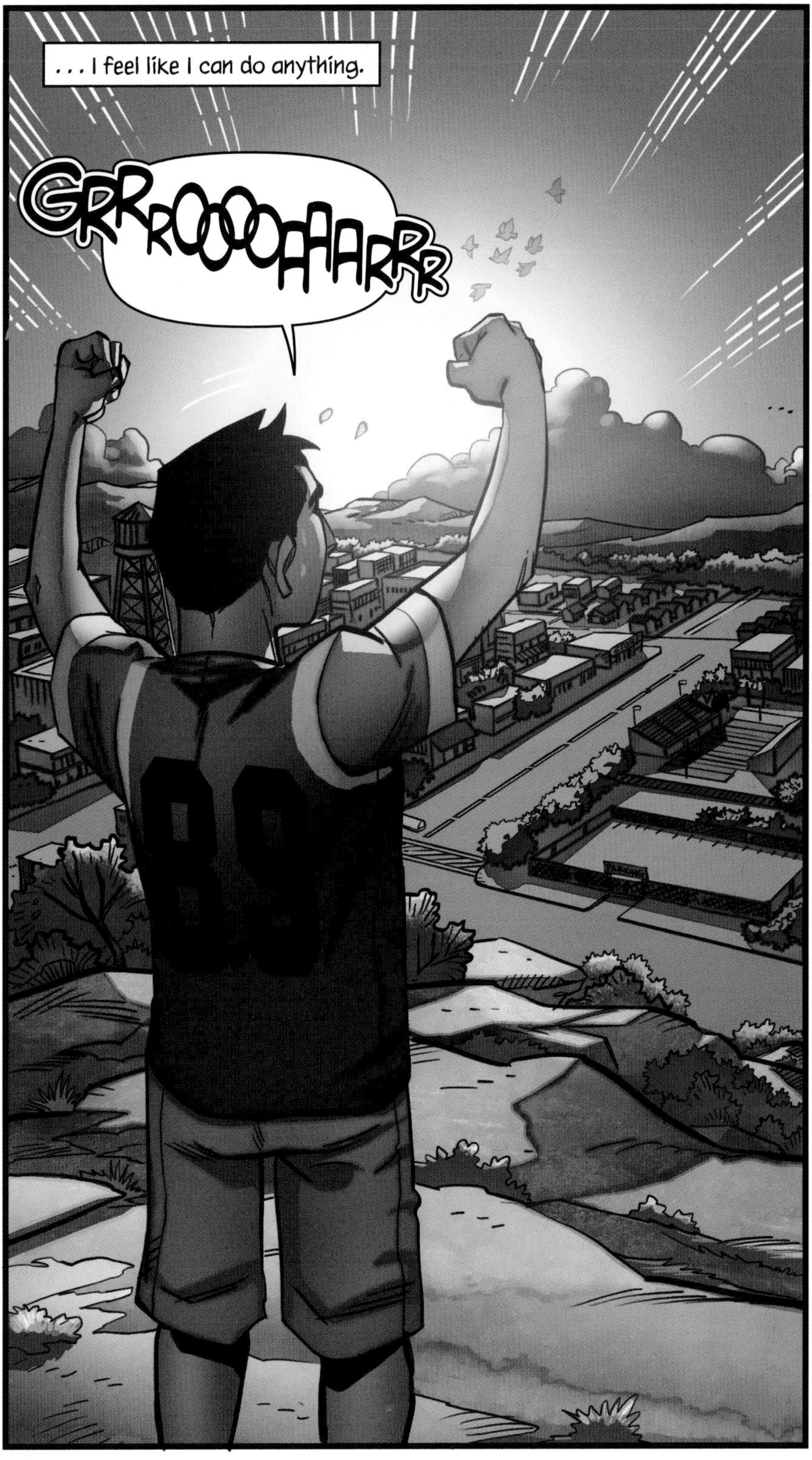
. . . I feel like I can do anything.
GRRROOOOAAARRR

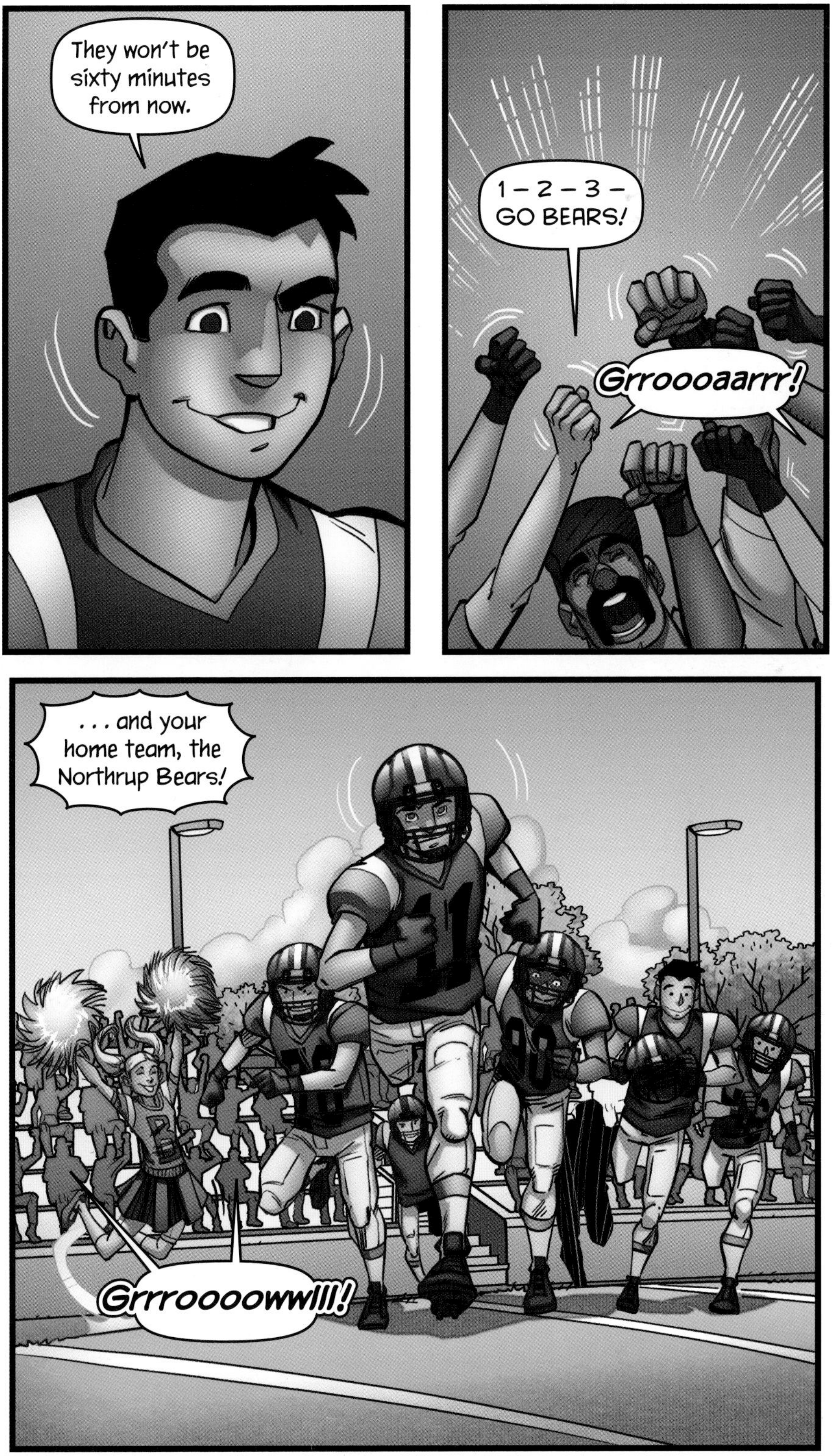
They won't be sixty minutes from now.
1 – 2 – 3 – GO BEARS!
Grroooaarrr!
. . . and your home team, the Northrup Bears!
Grrroooowwlll!

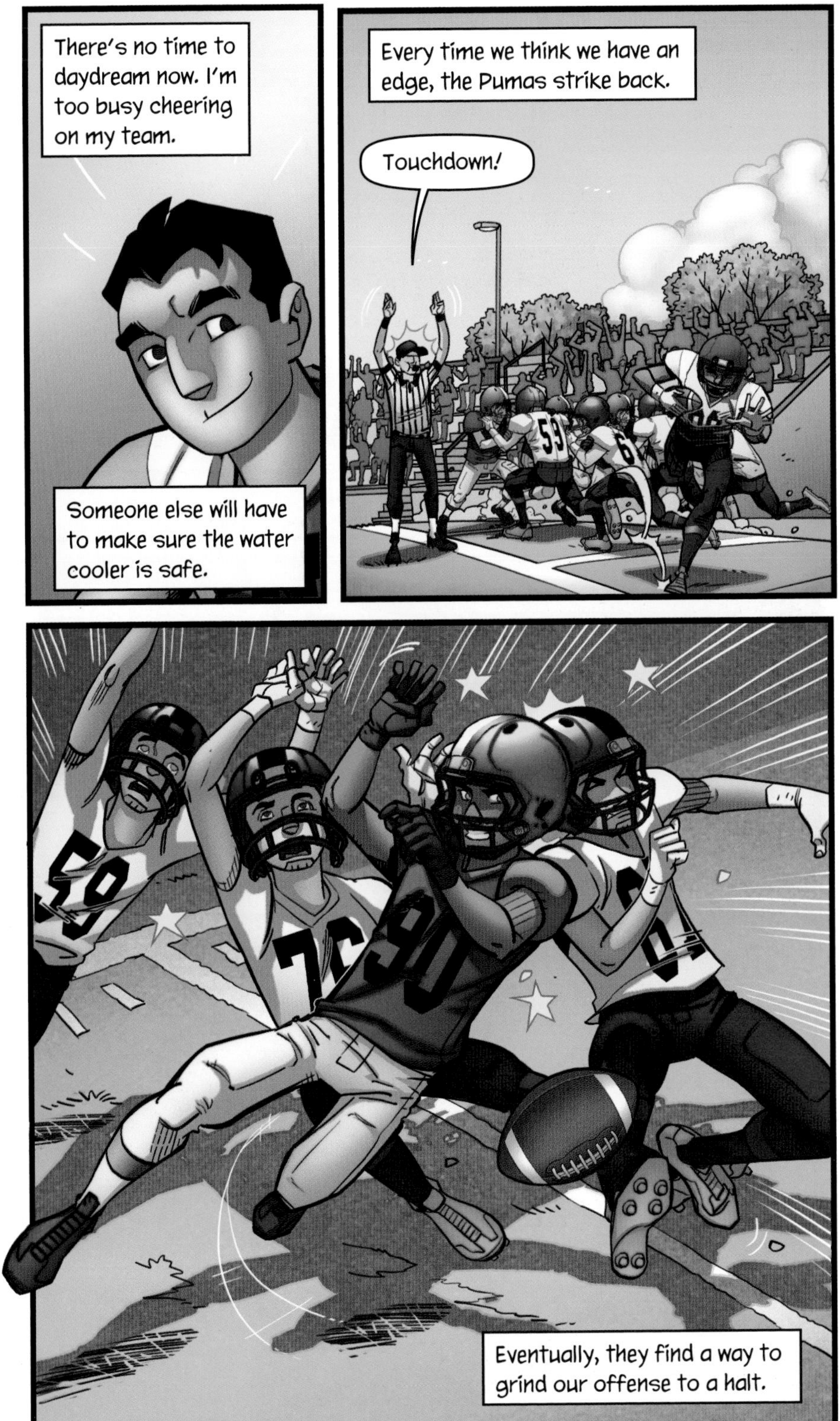
There's no time to daydream now. I'm too busy cheering on my team.
Someone else will have to make sure the water cooler is safe.
Every time we think we have an edge, the Pumas strike back.
Touchdown!
Eventually, they find a way to grind our offense to a halt.

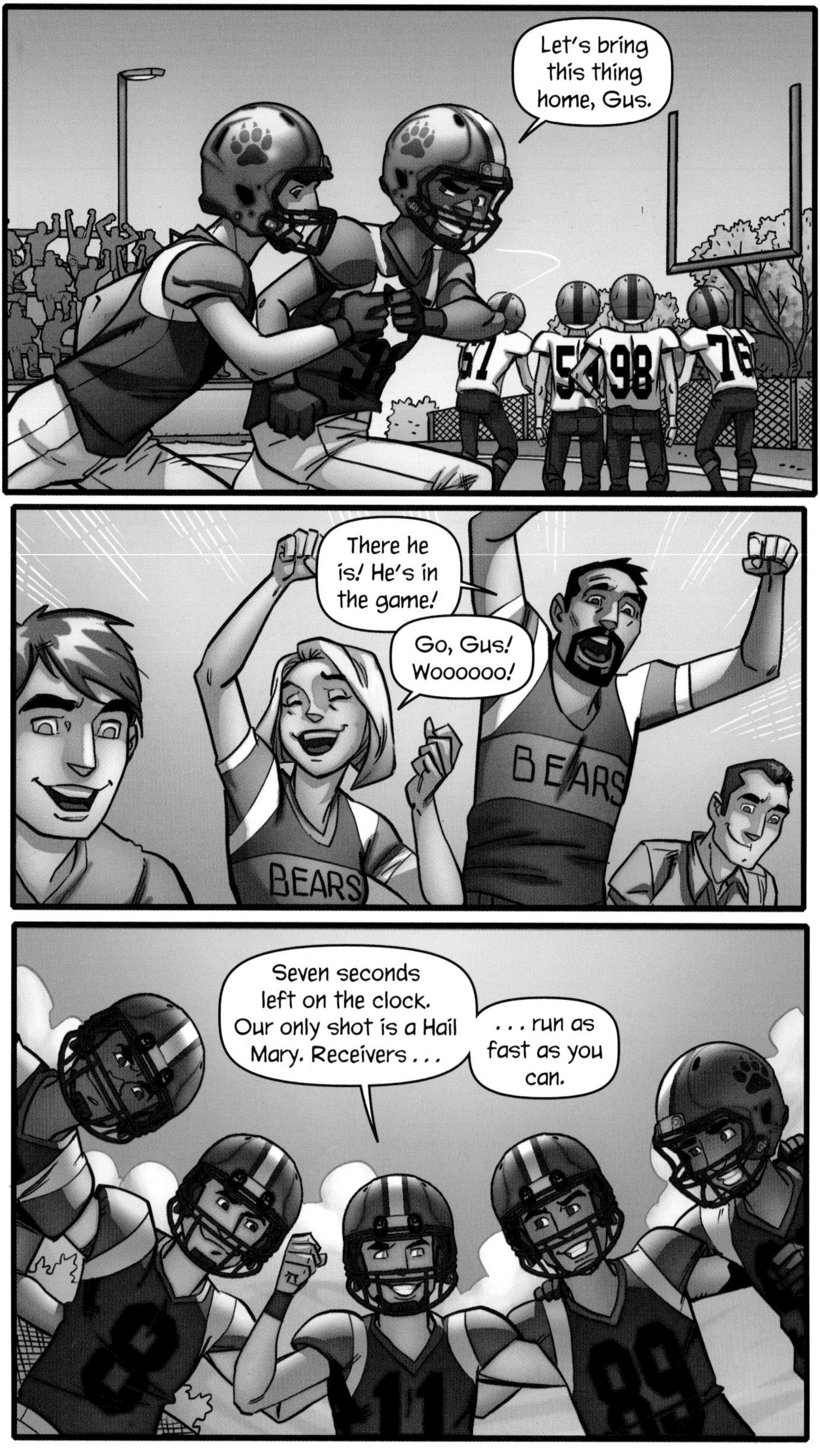

Let's bring this thing home, Gus.
There he is! He's in the game!
Go, Gus! Woooooo!
BEARS
BEARS
Seven seconds left on the clock. Our only shot is a Hail Mary. Receivers . . .
. . . run as fast as you can.

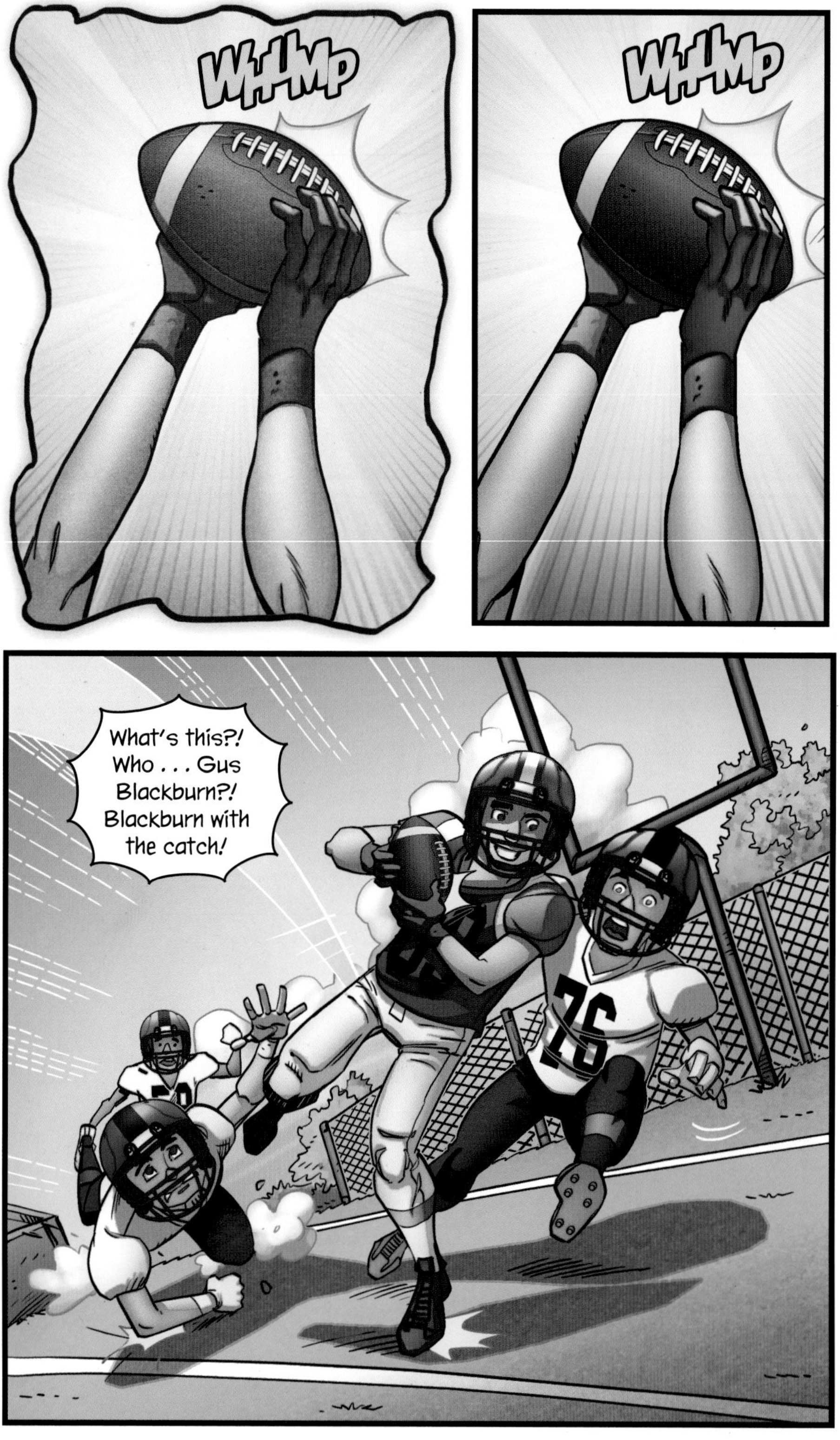
WHUMP
WHUMP
What's this?!
Who . . . Gus
Blackburn?!
Blackburn with
the catch!

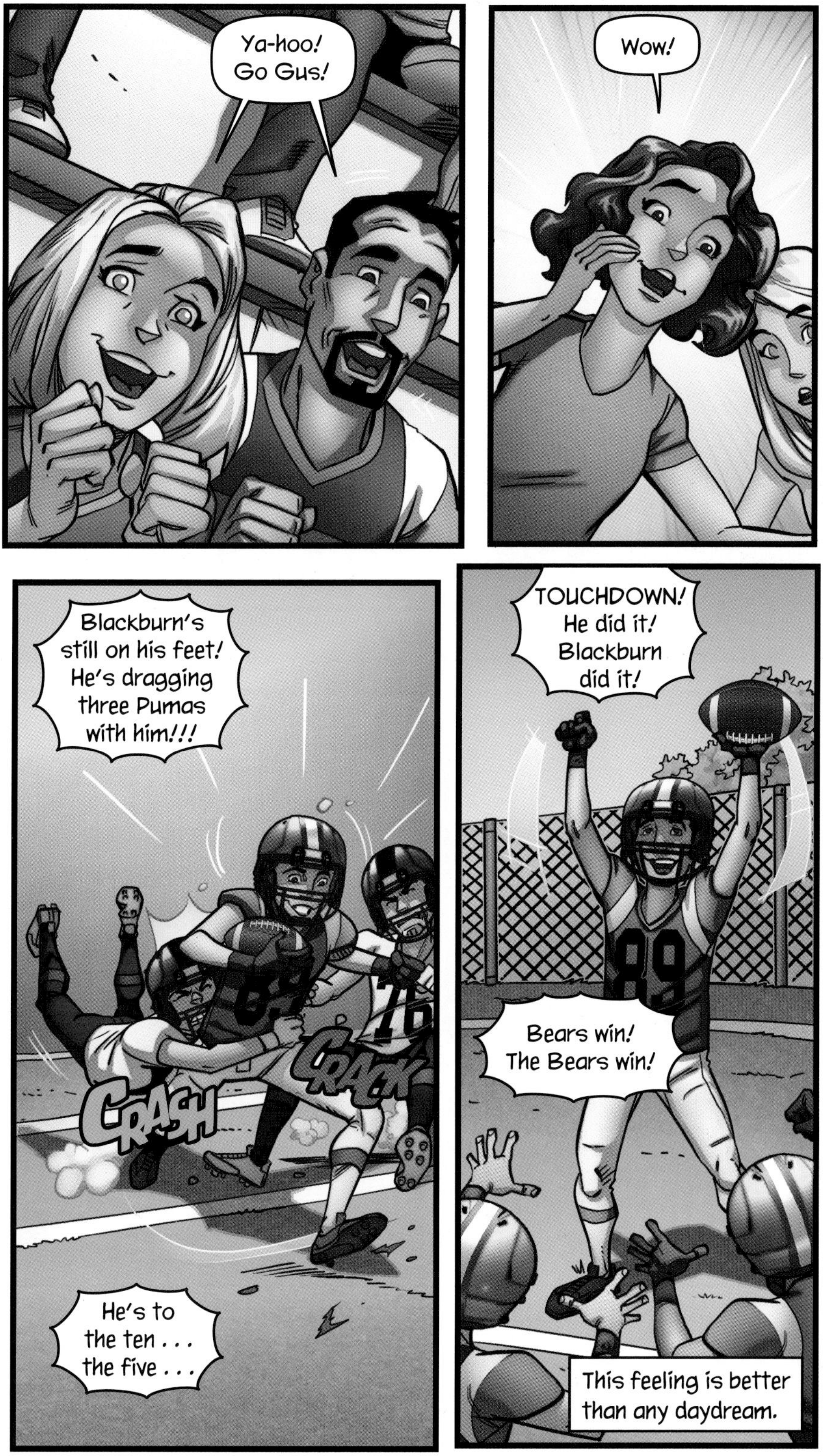
Ya-hoo! Go Gus!
Wow!
Blackburn's still on his feet! He's dragging three Pumas with him!!!
CRASH
CRACK
He's to the ten . . . the five . . .
TOUCHDOWN! He did it! Blackburn did it!
89
Bears win! The Bears win!
This feeling is better than any daydream.

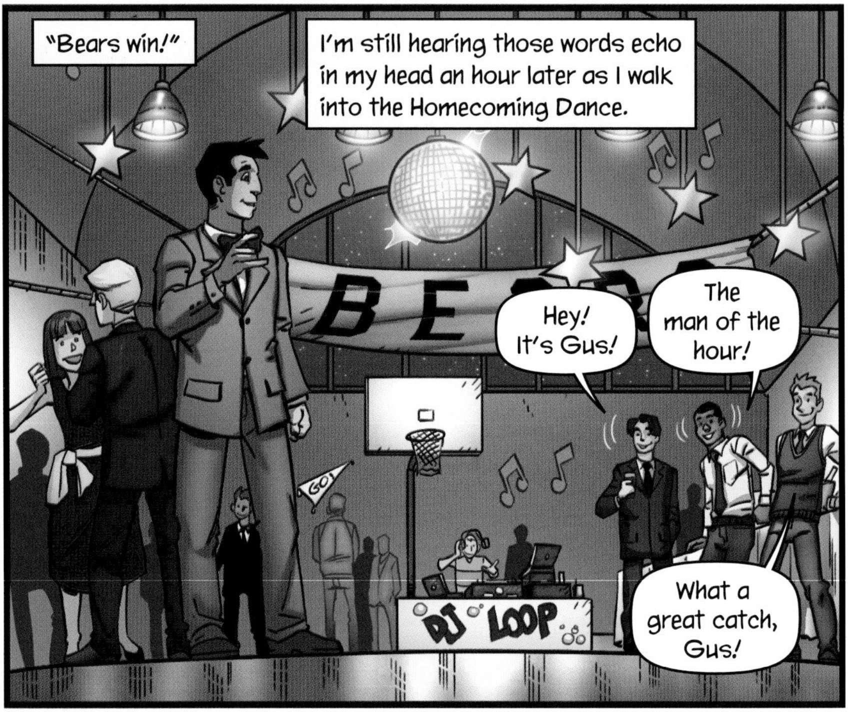
"Bears win!"
I'm still hearing those words echo in my head an hour later as I walk into the Homecoming Dance.
BE
Hey! It's Gus!
The man of the hour!
GO!
DJ LOOP
What a great catch, Gus!

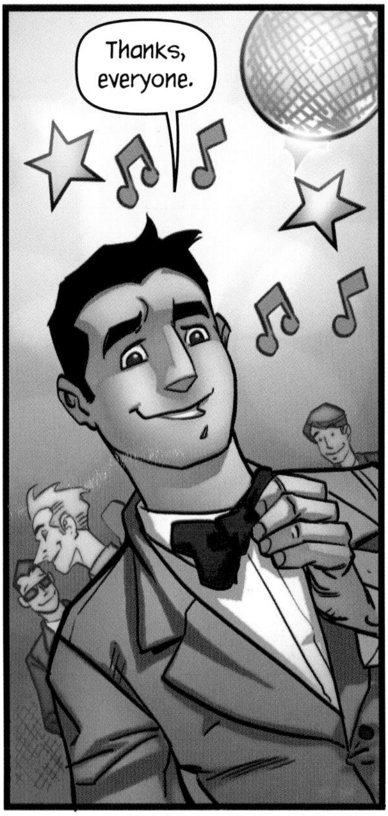
Thanks, everyone.

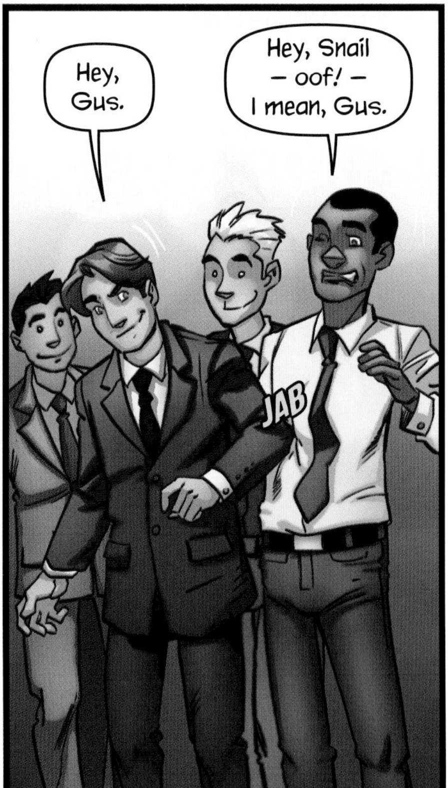
Hey, Gus.
Hey, Snail — oof! — I mean, Gus.
JAB

VISUAL
::::
QUESTIONS

1. Graphic novels use illustrations to show us how characters are feeling. How do you think Gus feels when his parents honk at him above, or as he stands alone on the street corner? Explain how the art helps to show his feelings in these two scenes.

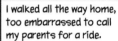

2. Graphic artists use various clues and art styles to tell a story. List the clues the artist used in this panel to show us that this is one of Gus' daydreams?

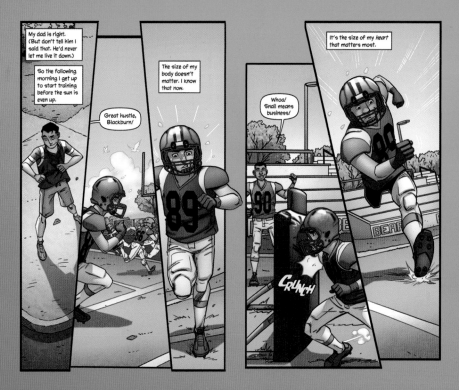

3. Study the above panels. What actions are being shown?
   Describe what's happening, and explain how these
   panels work together to push the story forward.

4. After Gus' heartfelt talk with
   his dad, he is determined to
   become the best player he
   can be. Look at the panel to
   the right. How does it show
   us Gus' new attitude and
   sense of purpose?

FOOTBALL POSITIONS

Football teams include both offensive and defensive players. During games, team offenses and defenses each have 11 players on the field at a time.

TEAM DEFENSE

The defense tries to stop the offense from advancing the ball and scoring points. Defensive players tackle opposing runners and try to knock down or catch the offense's passes.

DEFENSIVE TACKLES — the inner two members of the defensive line in charge of stopping running plays

DEFENSIVE ENDS — the outer two members of the defensive line in charge of holding the line of scrimmage

LINEBACKERS — usually the best tacklers on a team who must often defend against running plays as well as passing plays

SAFETIES — these players are the last line of defense and must defend against deep passes and running backs who get by the linebackers

CORNERBACKS — players who line up opposite the offense's wide receivers, they defend deep passes thrown toward the wide parts of the field

TEAM OFFENSE

The offense tries to run and pass the ball downfield to score points and win the game.

QUARTERBACK — the leader of the team who calls plays and yells signals to the team; this player hands the ball to a running back, throws to wide receivers, or runs with the ball

CENTER — the player who snaps the ball to the quarterback

RUNNING BACK — a player who runs with the ball

FULLBACK — a player in charge of blocking for the running back

WIDE RECEIVER — a player who runs downfield, evades defenders, and catches passes from the quarterback

TIGHT END — a player who lines up to the left or right of the quarterback and acts as a receiver and a blocker

LEFT AND RIGHT GUARDS — the inner members of the offensive line who block for the other players

LEFT AND RIGHT TACKLES — the outer two members of the offensive line

GLOSSARY

B-squad (BEE-skwahd)—a group of backup players on a sports team

cleats (KLEETS)—athletic shoes with rubber spikes or wedges on the soles that provide greater traction on grass fields

confidence (KON-fi-duhnss)—to believe in yourself and your own abilities

determination (dih-tur-muh-NAY-shuhn)—to continue trying to achieve a goal no matter how difficult it is

fly-pattern (FLY-PAT-uhrn)—a route run in football in which the wide receiver runs straight upfield toward the end zone

Hail Mary (HAYL MAY-ree)—a play where the quarterback throws the ball deep toward the end zone in the hope that one of the team's receivers will catch it

humiliation (hyoo-mih-lee-AY-shun)—to be made to feel ashamed or foolish by someone else

interception (in-tur-SEP-shun)—a pass caught by a defensive player

milestone (MILE-stone)—an important event or development

playbook (PLAY-book)—a notebook containing descriptions of the plays and strategies used by a sports team

scrimmage (SKRIM-ij)—a practice game

volatile (VOL-uh-tuhl)—unstable or explosive

READ THEM ALL!

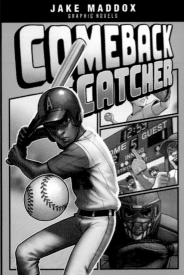

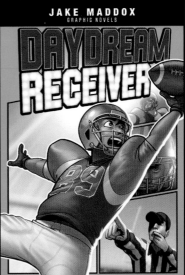

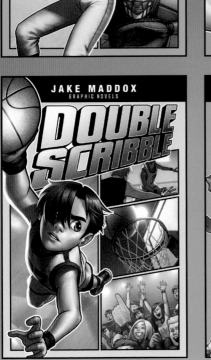

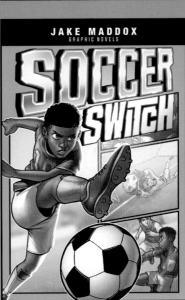

FIND OUT MORE AT
WWW.MYCAPSTONE.COM

BRANDON TERRELL

ABOUT THE AUTHOR

Brandon Terrell is the author of numerous children's books, including several volumes in both the Tony Hawk 900 Revolution series and the Tony Hawk Live2Skate series. He has also written several Spine Shivers titles, and is the author of the Sports Illustrated Kids: Time Machine Magazine series. When not hunched over his laptop, Brandon enjoys watching movies and TV, reading, watching and playing baseball, and spending time with his wife and two children at his home in Minnesota.